I0717709

Also available from Lion's Share Press

The Darkness of Shadows
Where the Devil Dwells
Metahumans vs Robots
Metahumans vs the Ultimate Evil

**Lion's Share Press
Moose Jaw, SK
CANADA**

This book is a work of fiction. Sadly, as cool as it would be, names, characters, places and events are either products of the author's imagination or used fictitiously. Any resemblance to actual events, humans, metahumans, metavillains, living, dead or undead, robots and/or androids or were-creatures is purely coincidental.

ISBN: 978-1-988163-05-5

PUBLISHED BY LION'S SHARE PRESS
www.LionsSharePress.com
www.Nightcat.ca
Text set in Georgia. Printed and bound in the USA.
Cover by J.L. MacDonald
Stock photos from 123rf.com

Contents

Introduction

We're taking a departure from the norm in that this is the first Nightcat short story anthology. Long-time readers may recognize some of the stories from other non-Lion's Share Press anthologies, but there are some here that haven't been published previously. I'd like to say they were written exclusively for this compilation, but I'd be lying.

Years ago I had an idea for a story and pitched it to Jim Robb for feedback. The idea was in the course of the series, time doesn't really pass and as such and I wanted to tell the story leading up to Nightcat's passing. Jim loved the idea and asked if he could write it. I enthusiastically said yes. I revere his writing and to be able to read a Nightcat story without having to write it myself was a real treat.

That little nugget of an idea then spiralled and I started figuring out what her life would be like five years in the future and onward, leading up to the events in Jim's story. I wanted more short stories and novels out before this would see print so I wrote it in between other projects whenever I got new ideas.

About a year or two ago there was a call for young adult short stories where the proceeds would go to charity so I volunteered to write one. Wanting to have the character be more identifiable with a younger audience led me to write the short story about Nightcat's (future) daughter, Nightfall.

Another call went out for short stories where the proceeds would go to another good cause. They wanted a mystery story which gave me the opportunity to write another short story from a different character's point of view, this time David's.

So for old and new Nightcat fans alike, I hope you enjoy the stories. And just think of the convenience of having them all in one book and taking up less shelf space!

J.L. MacDonald

J.L. MacDonald

Night(Cat) of the Living Dead

I wish physical violence was rare in my line of work, but sadly, that's not the case. Thankfully this time there wasn't an overabundance of it.

I was out on one of my nightly romps when I came across something that could potentially be trouble. A well dressed man was being approached by a shabby, gangly looking individual. His body language told me he was planning something, likely figuring out a way to rob the man, with or without a fight.

I swung into action just as he lunged and unexpectedly sank his teeth into the side of the other man's neck. I wasn't sure what to make of it, but I didn't have time to analyze the situation. My cat-like feet made contact, sending him flying to the other end of the alley way. I expected him to either lay there unconscious or scramble to his feet and flee. Instead he glared at me intently, then slowly stood up and casually walked away as if nothing happened.

I normally would have gone after him but the other man needed my help. I couldn't judge how deep the wound was because of the blood, but I knew he needed more medical attention that I could offer.

"Do you have a cell phone?" I asked.

He nodded and tried to grab it off his belt.

"Don't worry, the ambulance will be on its way," I attempted to reassure him as I tried to further assess the damages. I ripped off a piece of his coat and used that for a bandage as my skimpy costume would have been inadequate for the job.

I phoned 911 and gave them all the details I could. Thankfully the ambulance arrived quickly. The medics put him on a stretcher, wheeled it into the ambulance and drove away, leaving the police behind to get a statement.

As I was talking to them, an unmarked police car rolled up and I knew it was David.

"It was really weird," I told him. "He didn't go after the victim's wallet and he didn't appear to be armed or anything. It was like there wasn't even a motive."

"Well, sometimes the motive is being in the wrong place at the wrong time," David replied as he jotted down what I said.

"I know, but it doesn't make any sense."

"Not all crimes do."

I looked quizzically at David.

"This isn't the first time this has happened," he explained. "Over the past month there have been similar reports of a person getting bitten by a tall, lanky individual. And more often than not, we end up finding a corpse not too far away from the incident."

"How come you never told me about this before?" I inquired.

David smiled as he placed a hand on my shoulder.

"Because I didn't want you to panic."

"The whole idea of me having you as my police contact is so I can help you guys out," I half joked, knowing that it wasn't the only reason why David and I got along so well. "Did you need me for anything else?"

"We've got a few more things to do around here, but you're good to go," David said. "See you later tonight, then?" he whispered so only I could hear. No one knew that we were in fact dating. Or more accurately, that David was dating my alter ego.

"Actually, Rach is coming over for a girls' night," I explained.

"Right, I forgot you mentioned that the other day. Well then, I won't intrude on your 'chick flicks'."

There was hardly any chance of that happening. Granted, I wasn't sure what movies Rachel would bring over, but I was quite certain they wouldn't be anything remotely akin to a romantic comedy.

Saying goodbye as Nightcat was always a challenge. We stood there awkwardly for a moment when normally we would have kissed. Even though just saying goodbye seemed so casual, it would have to do.

Once I got home, I changed into my human self and took a quick shower, not having sufficient time for my usual hour-long soak in the tub.

Rachel came by shortly after I was finished.

"I'm actually impressed you're here," she joked as she tossed several DVDs on the coffee table.

"Hey, I've been good lately," I retorted. Rachel was one of the few people who knew about my other identity and how it was increasingly hard for me to keep appointments because of it. Even though it bothered me to no end, she never seemed to mind.

"So what movies did you bring over?" I asked as I thumbed through the video lineup.

"Before you say anything, I've watched them before and they're good movies," she said in mock defence.

I read the titles. "1001 Ways to Kill a Zombie", "The Monster Trials" and "Inside Frankenstein's Briefcase".

I let out an inaudible groan when Rachel sat down on the couch beside me.

"If I can watch them, you can watch them," she said referring to the gore level.

Horror movies never made me queasy, they just weren't my kind of movie. But tonight I'd humour her. Or at least try to.

It was pretty close 1 AM by the time we were finished the first two movies. Rachel fell asleep halfway through the last one so I shut it off and let her crash on the couch.

Even though I wasn't overly tired, I still got ready for bed. My body had long gotten used to staying up late thanks to my feline half. As I sat in bed, trying to wind down, I couldn't help but think how similar the movies were to what I encountered earlier in regards to the sheer randomness of it all. I briefly mulled it over in my head before drifting off to sleep.

* * *

The next few days were fairly normal, but when David phoned me at the office asking for Nightcat's help, I knew things weren't too normal for him.

"I'm really sorry to bother you at work, Dana. I wouldn't have called if I didn't need you," he said apologetically.

"Don't worry about it," I replied. "What's up?"

"You remember that incident a few days ago?"

"Yeah."

"Well, it turns out it's happened a few more times since then."

"*What?*" I asked incredulously.

"Things have been getting weirder and weirder. The man that you saved last week went missing from the hospital early this morning. The most we can piece together is that he attacked several orderlies and ran off. We've searched high and low but haven't got any leads on his whereabouts."

"And you want me to find him?"

"Actually, I wanted your insight for something else." David hesitated for a moment before continuing. "These incidents are happening more and more often. People are getting attacked and, more often than not, bitten. One person even succumbed to his injuries and his body went missing from the morgue. We looked at the security footage but there wasn't anything useful. You see how weird this is?"

David was obviously at a loss. He was an experienced cop, but his frustration was understandable given the circumstances.

"I'll certainly do whatever I can to help."

"I'd really appreciate it, Dana."

I smiled. David knew there wasn't anything I wouldn't do for him.

"Did you want me to meet you at the station after work?" I asked.

"I know you can't keep missing work on my behalf, so whenever you're able to get away at the end of the day would be fine."

"So what was your plan?"

"I was hoping to go back to a previous crime scene and backtrack from there. I was hoping you could try and pick up the trail of the attacker."

"I can certainly try, but I didn't exactly get a good scent." I may have heightened senses in cat-mode but some things you just don't notice. Unless the person had a unique smell or I was specifically trying to track someone, I didn't generally pay attention to it. Having acute senses can overload the brain so I learned to tune out the extraneous information.

"If that doesn't work, then maybe we can try the other locations?" David asked.

"Sure. I'll try to be over right after work."

"Thanks, Dana. I appreciate it," David said sincerely.

"You owe me," I joked.

"I always do," David laughed before he hung up.

I tried my best to concentrate on work the rest of the day, but I couldn't help my mind wandering. If David was confused over all of this, then understandably so was I. I only hoped I could help him.

As Nightcat, I met David in his office shortly after 5:30 and we went over all the evidence so far. The morning's phone call summarized it, but now David gave me the gritty details.

After the short briefing we drove to the place where the assault occurred. I attempted to let my senses guide me so I scented the air more than I usual.

"Getting anything?" David asked.

I shook my head. "Not really. It's pretty dank around here so it's hard for anything else to come through. That and I don't exactly know what I'm looking for."

David came over and patted me on the shoulder. "Regardless, I'm still glad you came."

"You can thank me after I've found whatever it is we're looking for," I smiled, then went back concentrating on the task at hand. I still didn't smell anything out of the ordinary so I tried doing a visual inspection. As I walked farther down the alley, I noticed a dishevelled man hunkered over by a dumpster, likely a homeless person trying to find something to eat.

"Excuse me," I asked as I gently tapped him on the shoulder. As soon as I made physical contact, I knew something was horribly wrong. My sixth sense reiterated that fact.

The man slowly turned around and grinned a toothless grin. His blank eyes stared right through me. I stepped back as he lumbered forward.

"Nightcat?" David asked in a stage whisper.

I didn't dare say a thing. And I didn't need to. Once David got a good look at this "thing" he knew something was wrong.

I continued to back step, staring at the monstrosity before me.

His grey saggy flesh hung loosely from the bones beneath. The eyes were a milky white, and it made me wonder how much he was able to discern. As he creaked forward, the panic rose in my chest. This being was vaguely human, but not quite. Almost like a poorly sculpted wax figure trying to get a tan.

David and I quite literally found ourselves up against the wall when several figures in the shadows started slinking forward. Something told me that they were much the same physically as the first creature.

"David?" I squeaked.

No answer.

I turned my head and saw David's eyes staring in disbelief.

"David!" I tried to bring him out of it.

"Sorry, I ... I don't know what to do, honestly," he stammered.

"And I'm supposed to?" I quietly chastised him.

No sooner did I finish my sentence than one of the monstrosities jumped me. As I struggled with my attacker, the rest of the horde grew closer. David shot a few of them in non-vital areas, but they kept coming.

It baffled me how something so lanky could actually be strong. I physically held his hands away from me, while he strained his neck getting closer to my face as he started snapping like an angry rabid dog.

Before David uttered his version of an expletive I heard the telltale sign of his gun clicking, indicating he was out of bullets. In that split second when I took my eyes off my attacker, he launched himself forward and took a chunk out of my neck with his teeth.

No amount of cursing was appropriate so I merely clutched my neck, trying to stop the bleeding.

"Come on, let's go!" David held out his hand and I accepted. Before I made it to my feet, David levelled one of the monsters with the butt of his pistol. Its skin ripped right along the cheekbone, but it didn't bleed.

David held my hand as we ran back to the vehicle. I took a quick glance behind and confirmed my worst fear: they were following and the ones in better shape were actually gaining on us.

David opened the driver's side door, pushed me into the car and jumped in after me. He slammed the door shut and hit the automatic locks as he started the engine. The freak show was attempting to surround the car. David slammed his foot down on the gas pedal so hard I thought his foot would go right through the firewall.

Several of the creatures got run over in the process, but when I looked in the side mirror, it didn't seem to deter them at all. Even though some of them were legless, they crawled forward in a last ditch effort.

"You OK?" David asked, his voice full of concern.

"I'm not sure," I said through gritted teeth.

I wasn't a stranger to pain, but this was different than anything I've ever felt before. And the wound wasn't healing as fast as it should have been.

"Let me see." David took his eyes off the road long enough to see the gaping hole in my neck. "We need to get you to a hospital."

"No, they won't be able to do anything," I said in a voice that barely sounded like my own.

"Dana, this is serious!" David exclaimed.

"You think I don't know that?" I said harshly. "Phone Raphael. Get me to the lab."

"Dana, no. There's no way ..."

"Just do it!" I demanded with more force than intended.

"You'd better know what you're doing," David grumbled as he made the call.

I closed my eyes for the remainder of the ride and concentrated on healing. For whatever good *that* would do me.

* * *

Raphael met us at the lab and gave me a quick going-over.

"It appears you have seen better days, Ms. Harker," Raphael smirked that annoying smirk of his. Leave it to him to be his annoyingly urbane self during something like this.

"Are you going to help me, or mock me?" I said quietly.

"I never mock, Ms. Harker," Raphael said deadpan. "Please, come with me."

Raphael escorted me to one of the lab's many observation rooms. Dr. Bertram was at his usual station in front of a giant monitor, his fingers typing away madly on the keyboard beneath.

He gave me one look and was in sheer shock.

"Might I ask what happened?" he asked as he showed me to the bed in the middle of the room.

It took every ounce of strength I had to hop up on the table. I removed my hand from the wound, which still hadn't healed.

"Let me get a sample," he said as he grabbed a Q-Tip and swabbed the area.

David stood by my side and squeezed my hand slightly.

It was a good thing I insisted on coming to the lab instead of the hospital. My healing factor would normally take care of any wounds I sustained, but this wasn't like anything I ever experienced.

"This doesn't look good," the doctor replied as he pushed his glasses farther up on his nose and scrutinized the readings on the monitor.

"What's wrong?" David asked the question for me.

"Whatever was in the saliva of the thing that bit you, is now causing the area to become necrotic and delaying your healing factor. I'm sure it will eventually heal itself, but by then it might be too late."

I flopped back onto the bed in utter defeat.

"Might I inquire the circumstances that brought this on?" Raphael looked down at David and asked.

Normally David wouldn't give in to one of Raphael's requests, but this was the exception to the rule. He recounted the events of the past several days.

"What were the defining physical characteristics of this fiend?" Raphael asked, pressing for more details.

"Why can't you forgo the formality and just ask me what he looked like?" I snapped.

"I believe I did," Raphael said smugly.

I closed my eyes and tried to bring up the mental picture of my attacker.

"His eyes were a milky white. Not like he had cataracts, but like he was blind," I recounted. "He was really thin, not an ounce of fat on him. His skin was hanging off his bones. That's all I remember."

"That almost sounds like ..." the professor started until Raphael interrupted him.

"Sounds like what?" I asked, not entirely sure I wanted the answer.

"It is nothing," Raphael waved it off, but I still wasn't convinced.

"It's not 'nothing'!" David said as he hit Raphael in the chest. He likely would have shoved him into the wall if Raphael didn't outweigh him threefold and wasn't a good foot and a half taller.

"Detective, please," Raphael said as he gently pushed David out of the way. When you had that kind of physical presence, you could pretty much get away with anything.

"Answer me, Raphael," David said through gritted teeth.

Dr. Bertram looked up at Raphael, who gave him a slight nod.

"During the early trials for the procedure, various pharmaceutical companies were interested in our findings, despite not being fully tested at the time," Bertram explained. "One of the first things we set out to do was create a healing factor in the test subjects. There was an anomaly in one of them and although we determined the root cause, it was too late."

"*More* test subjects? How many more people have you experimented on?" I demanded.

"'Test subjects' do not automatically imply they were human," Raphael interjected.

"They wouldn't be anymore," I grumbled.

"If you must know, Ms. Harker, they were lab mice." Raphael was getting increasingly frustrated with me.

Bertram continued. "Instead of a healing factor, one mouse had the opposite happen. In layman's terms, it started decaying from the outside in."

"Or to put it simply, you had a zombie mouse," I offered.

As soon as I made the connection, my mind went on a wild tangent. Zombies were supposed to be fictitious, yet the events happening around me were very real.

"So now what?" I asked Raphael. "I sit here and slowly rot to death?"

"Your healing factor has dealt with far worse situations."

"And I'm supposed to trust that the people that contributed to giving me a healing factor didn't screw that up too?"

"Ms. Harker," Raphael said gently. He was obviously trying to calm me down. "The faulty trial happened long ago. It has since been rectified and tested."

"On who?"

"You and I."

If I had any more energy, I would have continued with the verbal war with him.

"If it's any consolation, your healing factor is at least keeping it at bay," the doctor said as he read the results off the monitor. "I'll do another test in a half hour and see if your condition improves."

"What am I supposed to do in the meantime?" I growled.

"What were you planning on accomplishing while incapacitated? Grocery shopping?" Raphael mocked.

I growled a low growl that was almost out of the range of human hearing but I knew it would register on Raphael's bat-like ears.

"Firstly, you would concentrate on healing," Dr. Bertram piped up. Even Raphael looked on, so he obviously had no idea what the next step would be.

"I can take a sample of your blood now and another after you heal. By the process of elimination that *should* tell us more about how to cure this virus."

"So once again you want me to be the guinea pig?" I couldn't say I liked where this was going.

"You will, no doubt, heal from this, but unless we can analyze it, other people are at risk," the doctor explained.

"Fine, do what you need to," I said with resignation in my voice.

"There is one caveat, however," the doctor said, more muttering to himself than anyone in particular.

"Well?" I desperately wanted him to spit it out.

"It would be impossible to guess how long your healing factor would take to absolve you of this infliction, and in the meantime, many more people could be infected," Bertram droned on.

"If time is of the essence, than perhaps you could quickly explain your solution," Raphael interjected.

"The healing factor is largely dependant on adrenaline."

"So? Tell me something I don't know," I said harshly.

"I could inject you with epinephrine to increase your heart rate and jump start the healing process."

"I'm sensing a 'but' ..."

"It is not without risks. Side effects include anxiety, increased heart rate, headache and hypertension to name a few. I would also have to estimate the amount necessary to give to you. Your healing factor is still largely undocumented so your body's response is difficult to hypothesize."

"If you had stayed in the lab after your transformation, perhaps we would have a better idea on your capabilities," Raphael sneered.

I uncharacteristically ignored him looked over at David.

"I don't like any of this," he said with a grimace.

"Neither do it. But I've been through worse. I'm sure my healing factor can handle it," I said with feigned optimism.

I took a moment before turning to Bertram. "Let's do it before I change my mind."

I really wasn't looking forward to this. Oddly enough, even though a lot was at stake, I was more worried about the needles. Ever since the procedure that turned me into Nightcat, I've been *extremely* phobic of them, most likely due to Raphael ramming an elephant-sized needle into my midsection. I've never forgiven him for that.

David held my hand while Dr. Bertram drew blood. Unfortunately, I couldn't squeeze David's hand as much as I wanted because I would have crushed it. I couldn't help but watch Bertram prep the needle, but looked away just before he injected me. It didn't take long before the burning sensation of the healing process intensified. At least it was working.

Several intense minutes passed, my pumping heart overtaking my immediate thoughts. I was sure it would jump right out of my chest and across the room.

My grip on David's hand increased until he winced. I abruptly let go and sank my claws into the side of the bed frame. I could hear the metal complaining, but I didn't care. Better the examining table than David.

I tried my best to remain calm, which was a near impossible feat. I writhed around on the bed, growling and groaning in pain.

Eventually the pain did subside, slowly. I was sweating so profusely that even my fur couldn't absorb it all. Once the adrenaline wore off, I felt chilled, like I was getting over a bad flu. As my body relaxed, it ached from being so tense.

Doctor Bertram looked at my neck to assess the outcome.

"It appears to be healing," he said as he drew another vial of blood and compared it to the earlier sample.

"What are your findings, Doctor?" Raphael asked, barely giving him enough time to make any conclusions.

"We already knew the cause of the anomaly, so it should be fairly straightforward to find the antibody responsible for eradicating it." Bertram studied the monitors.

After a few minutes of silence, Bertram finally made the diagnosis known.

"The good news is that we can synthesize a cure. The bad news is that not everyone will respond to it."

"Please elaborate, Doctor," Raphael said.

"If a person is in an advanced state of decomposition, the cure will be useless."

"So what do we do with the badly infected people?" I asked.

"In order to prevent the spread of the virus, they must be destroyed," Bertram said without any emotion in his voice.

"So they need to be killed. Great," I muttered. "And what of the cure?"

"The best method would be to deliver it using the city's water supply," Bertram stated. "That way the rest of the population will gain immunity."

"And we need to kill the infected people why?" I asked.

"Do you wish more innocent blood to be shed, Ms. Harker?" Raphael asked.

"You know I can't kill those poor people," I shot back. "You might not have any problems with murder, but I do."

"What will happen to the infected if they're left alone?" David piped up.

"They will wither away and die a slow, agonizing death," Raphael replied. "You see, Ms. Harker, I am not without a conscience."

"Just because you claim to have one doesn't mean that you do," I snapped.

I still couldn't get over what they wanted me to do.

"And why can't you deal with them?" I asked Raphael. He may not have had my agility, but he more than made up for it in brute strength and had the power of flight, thanks to his 30 plus-odd foot wingspan.

"Do you wish to break into the water treatment plant to administer the cure?" Raphael asked.

I could have done it easily enough, but it wouldn't look good for both David and I to be caught breaking and entering. It was too risky.

It was like Raphael read my mind. Damn him.

"I am not in good favour with the law enforcement community, so I propose that I take this assignment while you and the good detective protect the public by ridding the city of the infected individuals."

I still didn't like the idea.

"I know what you're thinking, Dana," David said in a soothing voice. "But they are already dead and it's our job to protect the public."

"I know, but I still don't like the idea," I grumbled. "And it means that I have to face them again."

"If it will make you feel better, I can go alone," David offered.

"There's no way I'm letting you do by yourself."

"I appreciate the support, Dana, but please don't feel you have to do this for my benefit," he said comfortingly.

"Yes, I do. I'm not going to sit at home while you're out becoming zombie chow. You need my help."

I turned to Raphael. "Before we go out, I want David to have the treatment, just in case something happens."

"But of course," Raphael replied.

David gave me an ambiguous look and I wasn't sure what he was thinking.

"Dana, can I speak to you?" He turned to Raphael. "In private."

"You do not trust my motives, Detective?" Raphael mocked.

"Absolutely not," David spat.

I somehow got this funny feeling that I would have to play referee between them. Not that it was the first time, and certainly it wasn't going to be the last time either.

"David, I know Raphael hasn't given us much reason to trust him, but I think he's telling the truth," I stated. Granted, it was hard for me to take Raphael's word at face value, but it would be exponentially more difficult for David.

"What reason would Raphael have for this charade?" I asked, not giving David time to answer. "Raphael doesn't normally do stuff that would involve more work on his part."

"I guess so, but I still don't trust him," David grumbled.

"If it'll make you feel better, I can take the vaccine in human form," I offered.

"Such a course of action would be a necessity as your healing factor is not present when you are not in your feline form," Raphael interjected.

Thank you, Captain Obvious, I thought.

"Let me make one thing clear," David challenged Raphael, "I'm only doing this because I trust Dana's judgement, *not* because I trust you. And don't think you're off the hook for helping us."

"I shall think nothing of the sort," Raphael said with a false sense of surprise.

It didn't take long for the doctor to administer the vaccine. Thankfully I was already healed when I changed to my human self, because otherwise I would have been in a world of hurt. Quite literally.

"So did you have a plan in mind?" David asked me.

"Sort of, but I don't much like it," I frowned.

* * *

Unfortunately the only thing I could think of was using David as bait. The zombies had a tendency to group so the idea was to put David in their proximity and I would deal with the majority of them.

I was guessing that their increase of strength was due to their inherent lack of tactile sensory information. Because they didn't feel pain, they could exert themselves beyond the point where a normal person would stop. They also lacked a sense of self preservation so if they did something that damaged them, it didn't stop them.

It was definitely going to be a challenge, even for me. I've battled Raphael before and even with his healing factor, if I hit him hard enough, he would be down for at least a short period of time. These guys you'd have to decapitate or dismember. I *really* wasn't looking forward to this. I guess once all of this was over with I could thank Rachel for educating me in the ways of proper zombie killing by subjecting me to her horror movie addiction.

Normally if David was undercover, he'd assume a persona that would blend in. But this time we wanted him to stand out, and we figured he'd garner more attention by being decently dressed in the alleys of the rough neighbourhood.

I was clinging to the side of a building, providing the necessary lookout. It didn't take long before I saw someone in ragged clothes lumbering toward David. I was pretty sure it was one of the infected, since several other similarly dressed individuals were creeping out of the shadows behind him.

My heart rate increase as I prepared for the fight. I didn't normally have to wait for a physical altercation to start, so in more ways than one, this whole experience was a first for me.

David kept his cool, trying to look as casual as possible. I'm sure his heart was beating as fast as mine, but he was far more used to covering it up than I was.

It didn't take long before David gave me the signal.

I launched the grappling hook from my right wrist cuff and it went right through one zombie's head like a bullet. It was hard to tell if he was *dead* dead because he stood there, flailing about with only half a face.

My sense of accomplishment was quickly diminished by another zombie grabbing the end of the grapple and heaving on it so hard that it make me lose my grip. I came crashing to the ground and I tried to concentrate on healing as fast as I could. I was already tagged by one zombie and I wasn't going to let it happen again. I shook my head as I rose to my feet and saw David running back toward me.

I only had enough time to react. I whipped my zombie skewered grappling hook at the one closest to David. The two dead bodies collided with a menacing thud. The one was down for the count, but the other was attempting to stand up. I didn't give him the chance.

I spun around on one foot, knocking his legs from beneath him. I evidently kicked him too hard because his legs snapped off like toothpicks and landed a good ten feet away.

When I recoiled my grappling hook, the attached zombie head exploded in a splatter of blood, and I whipped it at the newly amputated zombie, tearing him in half.

While I had saved David from that zombie, more were closing in on him. Only one thought came to mind and I was sure David wouldn't like it.

It only took two short bounds to get close to him. I fended off the nearest attackers, picked David up, and sprinted to the nearest dumpster.

David's going to kill me, I thought. *But at least he'll be safe.*

I opened up the dumpster, gently tossed David in and closed it behind him. Just to make sure no walking undead got to him before me, I gripped the lid as hard as I could, crimping it to the front wall of the container. I was certain the zombies couldn't open it and get to him.

"Nightcat!" David shouted from inside and he banged on the walls as hard as he could. "LET ME OUT!!!"

"I will!" I hollered back, "As soon as I'm done killing these things off."

I'm sure David wasn't thrilled about being in such a wretched-smelling place, but at least I could concentrate on killing the zombies permanently and not worry about David's safety. I could go all out on the slaughterfest.

David kept banging and screaming my name, but I was too busy to respond.

When I turned around, I was faced with an almost completely intact individual. He must have been recently infected because he still retained many human features, albeit looking a little anemic.

"I've never liked cats," he hissed. "Evil little creatures they are."

"I bet you say that to all the girls." As I spoke, I mentally geared myself up to take him down. He'd likely prove more of a challenge than the others. He was so human-like by comparison that I'd have a hard time psychologically coming to grips with it. For the first time, I felt a twinge of envy for Raphael's amorality.

I wanted to avoid getting too close, so I jumped up onto the side of the building, claws digging into the brickwork. I scurried over to the fire escape and yanked two metal balusters off the guard rail.

"If you're trying to scare me, it isn't working," he said smugly.

I had initially thought of beating him with the metal rods, but a better plan came to mind.

Holding one like a javelin, I launched it in his direction. He may have been faster than his buddies, but even a living athlete would have had problems getting out of the way fast enough.

The twisted metal rod went through his left eye socket and hit the building behind it. He was brought to his knees, yet still had some undead life in him.

To make sure it would cause more damage, I bent the metal rod into the shape of a ball and hurled it at his torso, taking a large chunk out and putting him down for the count.

There was a couple more contenders waiting on the sidelines. I wasn't sure if they were actually mulling the idea in their minds or if they were waiting for me to make the first move.

As much as it disgusted me, I knew I would have to go hand to hand with them. The thought sent a cold shiver down my spine.

With one last fleeting thought of how long it would take to wash the rotting flesh odour out of my fur, I leapt towards one of them and before he had time to react, I ripped his arms right from the socket, and shoved one through the fleshy part under the jaw and into what was left of his brain.

My sixth sense warned me that one was in close proximity. I knew he was behind me from the direction of the scent. I knocked his legs out from under him with my tail, and using the other dismembered arm, drove it into his mouth and through the other end of his skull.

I was reacting so much on instinct that when I turned around to meet the newest attacker, I realized there was none. All I heard was David screaming and banging on the dumpster.

"I'm coming!" I shouted, hoping he could hear me.

He continued to bang on it, so much so that I was getting a tinnitus from the noise.

"I'm here, David, I'm here." He must have heard me because the noise instantly stopped.

I ripped open the dumpster lid and David sprung up like a jack-in-the-box.

"What the *hell* were you thinking?" David chastised me as he wiped off the remnants of someone's bagged leftovers.

I had to take a step back. The smell was so intense that I was afraid I'd throw up.

I coughed a few times before answering him.

"I'm sorry." I coughed a few more times. Evidently it wasn't out of my system. "It was the only thing I could think of to keep you safe."

"And for that I thank you, but do you have any idea how long it'll take me to wash this stuff off? Eau de dumpster is very hard to get out."

"Perhaps, but I'd be willing to help you with that," I half joked. "I mean, it's my fault that you smell like a vomiting skunk."

"So I guess this means that you got them all." David looked around as he continued to pull day-old spaghetti from his hair.

"I think so. Doesn't look like there are any other contenders."

"So now what?" David asked.

"I guess we call Raphael up so he can dispose of the bodies," I shrugged. "I'm sure as hell not cleaning that mess up!"

"But yet you can put up with cleaning up my mess?" David joked.

"I guess we'll find out," I said.

Marked For Death

"Umm, hi?" David said as I practically flew into his office. I slammed the door behind me and quickly closed the blinds.

"Nightcat, are you OK?" he asked with a small bit of panic and a lot of confusion in his voice.

I took a second to calm myself before answering him. "I think so. I'm not sure."

"So which is it?"

"Physically, I'm fine. Just a little shaken up, that's all," I replied. I leaned back on his desk, but my arm gave way. "OK, I lied," I said as I grabbed my aching shoulder.

David came closer and put his hand on mine.

"Can I have a look?" he asked gently.

"Sure, but I doubt you'll find anything," I said as I removed my hand to reveal nothing but the chocolate brown fur underneath.

David gently pushed his fingers into the muscles of my shoulder, obviously trying to find the source of the pain.

"What happened?" David asked as he kept prodding.

"I was out and about when I came across some guy getting beat up in an alley. I dove in and when I apprehended the mugger, my sixth sense went off," I explained. "And it wasn't because of him either. I moved out of the way but a bullet grazed me."

"Did you see who shot you?"

I shook my head. "No, it was just me, the mugger and the guy he beat up. I couldn't see anyone else. I knocked the mugger out and ran off behind another building and out of sight. My sixth sense was still warning me of something, but it wasn't as strong as it was before."

"The bullet more than just grazed you. I think I can feel it," David said as he pushed his fingers deeper into my shoulder. I winced a little, but I was also no stranger to pain. "I think your body healed itself with the bullet still inside."

I slumped over. "Wonderful."

I've been in a similar situation before and knew I had to extract the bullet myself. I unsheathed the claws on my left hand and mentally prepared myself.

"Dana, don't you think we should take you to the hospital? They can at least freeze the area," David suggested.

I looked up at David and placed my hand on his cheek.

"I appreciate the gesture, but remember the last time I went to the ER? They patched me up but it was an administrative nightmare. As far as they're concerned, I'm not even from Ontario, let alone Canada. Ergo, I don't qualify for free health care."

"I suppose. I don't have to like it though," David said solemnly. He liked seeing me in pain almost as much as I liked *being* in pain. "Stay here, I'll grab the first aid kit."

I was about to protest until I realized that I would need something to soak up the blood I'd lose while my body was healing itself.

In David's absence, I poked and prodded my shoulder to try and get a good idea of where exactly the bullet was. I couldn't feel it so much as the pain of the tissue being pressed into it.

David returned a moment later with Inspector Sorowski in tow.

"What the hell happened, Cat?" he asked gruffly. I quickly told him what I knew.

"Don't worry, I'm fine. Much to your dismay," I quipped.

"You damn well better not bleed all over the place." That was Sorowski's way of expressing concern.

David set the med kit on his desk, opened it up and grabbed some gauze. "Why don't you sit in my chair?" he asked.

"Yeah, it might be easier," I said as I sat down.

"I hope you're not squeamish," I said to Sorowski as I unsheathed my claws.

He stood there, arms crossed and I didn't wait for a reply. Instead I took a deep breath before plunging my claws into my shoulder. I let out a little growl as I dug deeper. David was close by, gauze in hand, to catch any dripping blood.

Thankfully it didn't take long to find the bullet, although when I did, the blood made it difficult to get a good grip. I fished around a bit more until I was finally able to ease it out.

David caught the bullet in one hand and applied the gauze to my shoulder with the other.

"It's OK, David. I got it," I said as I placed my hand on his and instantly regretted it. I tried my best not to let my feelings show for him when I was in cat form. Only a few people knew I had a secret identity, and Sorowski wasn't one of them. I didn't want him to figure out that David and I were, in fact, dating.

David just looked at me and showed a hint of a smile before pulling his hand away and looking down at the bullet.

"That's odd," he murmured.

Before Sorowski could even get a word in, I piped up. "What is?"

"It doesn't look like a lead bullet." David scrutinized the bullet fragment further.

Sorowski got in for a better look, and grabbed his glasses from his breast pocket. I showed great restraint by not mocking him.

"It looks like it's made out of something harder than lead. This is still very bullet shaped," Sorowski commented.

I slid farther down in the chair. "Let me guess. It's silver."

"Possibly," David said as he looked up at me. I answered him even before he asked the question.

"Lucky guess," I sighed. "Someone obviously thought silver bullets would work on a werecat in the same way as it would a werewolf."

"Werecat?" Sorowski asked as he tucked his glasses away in his grey sports jacket.

Panic rose in my throat. I had pretty much insinuated that I could change back and forth.

"For lack of a better word," David piped up. "Obviously she isn't a human who turns to a cat during the full moon, or she'd be human now."

I instantly relaxed and made a mental note to thank David later.

"I imagine you didn't get a good look at the guy who shot you?" Sorowski asked.

"Am I being interrogated?" I half joked.

"It'll be pretty hard to bring the guy to justice if no one saw him."

"Well, next time someone tries to kill me, I'll remind myself to get a good look at his face," I said sarcastically.

"Any ideas who'd want you dead?"

"Uuuh, pretty much anybody I've sent to jail?" That was a pretty dumb question to ask, even for Sorowski.

"I'm trying to help you out, Cat," he chastised. "I'd like to know what the motive might be. You're used to people shooting at you, but a perp being that secretive about it? Now that I find odd."

"Maybe he was scared that if he missed I'd get pissed off and go after him?" I suggested.

"Just promise me the next time you're out, you'll be careful?"

I laughed. "Don't tell me you're concerned for my welfare, Sorowski?"

"I look out for all the guys on my watch."

"Last time I checked I wasn't a guy. Nor was I on your watch." Technically I wasn't a police officer but I did hold an honorary rank, and was more or less partnered with David on an unofficial basis. It was nice now that I didn't have to try and convince the cops I was on their side. Granted, there were still some on the force that gave me a hard time, but it was still a relief to know that the police wouldn't shoot me down on sight because of the way I looked. Even David hadn't been sure what to make of me the first time we met. Not that I blamed him, of course. Saving him from being murdered by a couple of drug dealers had upped my PR a notch or three, though.

"How are you feeling?" David asked.

I removed the gauze and watched the wound repair itself.

"I thought you healed faster than that?" Sorowski asked.

"Sometimes," I replied. "It's largely dependant on adrenaline."

Normally I didn't care to discuss my strengths and weaknesses with anyone other than close friends, but I also knew that Sorowski wasn't about to use it against me.

"A few more minutes and I should be right as rain," I said to Sorowski, hoping he'd leave us.

He gave us both a quick look. "I'm glad you're OK," he said before heading out.

David closed the door behind him.

I looked at the hole in my shoulder, but it was pretty much gone. Only a scab remained, and I knew it wouldn't be much longer before that healed and my fur would grow back, leaving no trace of any injury.

David massaged it lightly with his hand and I knew what he was thinking. I grasped his hand in mine and looked up at him.

"You're OK?" David asked gently, even though he already knew the answer.

I gave him a quick kiss on the lips.

"You worry too much," I replied.

"I'm allowed," David smirked. "So, you have no idea who it *might* have been?"

"Not really. Granted, I hadn't thought much about it ..."

"My gut tells me Raphael had something to do with it."

I laughed, even though it wasn't the best reply. Raphael, a seven and a half foot tall humanoid bat that put Mr. Universe to shame, was the one who had mutated me. A part of me would never forgive him for putting me through that hellish procedure, but as time went on I found myself hating him less and less. David, on the other hand, had a hard time letting go. I found it odd that I was increasingly able to forgive Raphael, but David and my friends and family weren't.

"David, you can't blame Raphael for *everything*," I said gently.

"But ..." David started but I brought my finger to his lips and smiled.

"I know," I said. "I know. You don't like him, and I don't blame you."

David grasped both my hands in his. "I don't understand it. If anyone should hate him, it should be you."

"And I do. Just not as much as the rest of you," I said softly. "Like I keep saying, I didn't like what he put me through and how he used me, but I'm beginning to see that the pros outweigh the cons."

"I suppose." David held me tight. "I still think he's involved somehow."

"I don't think so. Raphael would never try to get rid of me so discreetly. If he was truly pissed off at me, he'd kill me himself. With his bare hands."

I had super-strength, but Raphael was still stronger. My level-headedness, agility and speed made me more of a contender, but one on one I doubted I'd stand a chance. Only when truly angered did my strength level even come close to his.

"I still think we should have a talk with him," David said, and I had to agree, if for no other reason than to see what Raphael knew or could find out about the situation.

"Mind if I use your phone?"

"Not at all," David said as he let me go.

I quickly dialled Raphael's cell phone instead of any of his other contact numbers. There weren't too many people that knew of our involvement and I wanted to keep it that way.

"Detective?" Raphael answered, obviously thinking it was David calling him.

"No, it's me."

"Ah, yes. Always a pleasure," his said in that annoying calm voice of his. I realized that, not knowing whether I was in my human or cat form, he was playing it safe. He had cleverness to go with his self-proclaimed genius-level intelligence.

"Look, I need your help."

He cut me off. "Always."

He was being far too nice and for a moment I wondered why.

"Can you meet me at my hideout in a half hour? It's not exactly something I want to talk about over the phone."

"I trust all is well?" I knew what he was getting at.

"Sort of. I mean, it's not life and death or anything," I said. "At least not yet. Can you meet me there or not?"

"But of course. I shall leave immediately." And with that he hung up.

"Goodbye to you too," I said into the dead handset.

"How are we going to work this out?" David asked. "I don't really think it's wise for you to be out as Nightcat right now."

I admired David for caring so much about my welfare, but sometimes he acted like an overprotective mother.

"Well, if I stay as Nightcat, I can sense danger. But whoever wants me dead wants Nightcat dead, not Dana Harker."

"True."

"But whichever form I take, I'll have the best security detail there is." I leaned closer, put my hand on the back of his neck and caressed his blonde hair.

I always had to be careful being touchy-feely with David when I was Nightcat, but I rather enjoyed it. My amplified senses made the experience that much more intense. I could hear his heart rate increase slightly, as well as his breathing.

"I guess we'd better head out," I said as I stood up. "If anyone asks, I came by to see you just as Nightcat left through your office window." Even after all this time it felt weird talking about myself in the third person.

David took a swig of what was left in his Timmie's mug before grabbing his coat.

"That's disgusting," I half joked. "The only thing worse than coffee is cold coffee." It was something I've never seen before. Coffee never lasted long enough to *get* cold when David was around.

"Waste not, want not. Besides, cold coffee is better than no coffee," David laughed as he put on his jacket.

"Have you eaten yet?" he asked.

"No. Why, what did you have in mind?"

"I was thinking we could pick something up along the way. It's Toonie Tuesday at Francine's House of Fries."

"Works for me," I replied as I started to change my appearance.   However   many   times   David   saw   the transfiguration, he was always in awe over it. I guess it would be spectacular for any onlooker, but it had long become second nature to me.

I started the change at my fingertips. The brown fur on my hands receded into the bare skin beneath. My metallic wrist cuffs melted away like they were liquid, and the fur was absorbed by my skin. My legs underwent the most drastic change, converting from the hind feet of a cat to regular jointed human legs. My tail gradually became shorter until it simply disappeared into my tailbone. Simultaneously, the hair on my head formed itself into my natural red coloured, shoulder length style. The last thing to undergo a change was my attire. While I couldn't morph partway, I could control where it started, which was usually my clothes. David had seen me in less coverage than my skimpy little costume so I didn't worry about feeling exposed. My black costume lengthened down my arms and thighs, simultaneously changing colour and texture back into what I had been wearing previously in my human form.

Not many people knew about my ability to transform, but I imagine if they did, I'd still be considered a werecat, even though the transfiguration was technologically based. The microscopic computers running in my bloodstream, nanites as Raphael called them, were able to structure my body back and forth between my human self and my cat form. I guess in some ways I could be called a shapeshifter, but I could only take the appearance of the two forms so I generally used the term "werecat".

* * *

A short while later we arrived at my hideout, which had been an old abandoned YMCA before I acquired it. At first I didn't see a real need for my version of a bat cave, but it had proved useful. David dubbed it "The Kitty Corner", probably just to see if he could get a reaction out of me. If it had been anyone else, I likely would have protested vehemently.

The common area was a big open space with a couple of gently used but comfortable couches and chairs, and a small kitchenette in one corner. While there were several more rooms in the building, this was generally where I spent my time when I needed to get away from everything.

Marginally tired, I decided to lie down on the couch for a bit and enjoy the peace and quiet while it lasted.

"Here, shove over," David said as he lay down next to me on the couch.

I rested my head on his shoulder and placed my hand on his chest. I didn't need enhanced senses to feel the rhythmic beating of his heart. I could have stayed like that for hours, but I heard the back door open.

I poked my head up over the back of the couch, and as expected, there was Raphael, in all his snooty glory.

"Don't you knock?" I chastised him.

"Had I known you were fornicating, I would have."

"We weren't screwing around," I yelled.

"Good. For a moment I thought you might have been unclad."

He was *really* starting to piss me off.

"Like I'd ever let you see me naked!"

"You flatter yourself, Ms. Harker. After all, I do have standards."

That did it. In a flash, I changed to Nightcat and launched myself at him, claws and fangs bared.

He sidestepped out of the way, and when I came crashing to the ground, he twisted my left arm behind me, preventing me from getting up.

My amber eyes quickly changed to green and back again as I growled at him. I heard what sounded like a firecracker going off and thought that David had fired a warning shot. When I twisted around I realized that it hadn't been a warning shot at all. He'd put a round into Raphael's right arm.

Raphael turned his attention to David, but I somersaulted to my feet and kicked him in the groin with my claws extended. In one bound I was in front of David in a defensive posture.

Raphael, doubled over in pain, glared up at me and let out an earth-shattering roar.

"You had it coming!" I snarled.

Raphael wasn't quite up to forming complete sentences yet. He just grumbled and growled for the next couple of minutes.

As soon as he staggered to his feet, I knew I hadn't done him any real damage. His healing factor worked like mine in that it would repair almost any damage as long as the body parts involved remained attached.

He lumbered closer while I continued to stand between him and David. I wasn't sure what Raphael would do next, but I certainly knew what he was capable of when angered. It had almost cost me my life once.

"Do you have *any* idea how infuriating that is?" he asked, his trademark accent distorted by anger.

"Not being a guy, no. But I imagine it wouldn't tickle," I stated. "It was the only way I could think of to stop you from going after David."

"Do you think so little of me, Ms. Harker, as to believe I would harm either of you? Especially when it was *you* who asked for *my* help," he grumbled.

"Look, I'm sorry," I said, only partially meaning it.

Raphael hobbled over to one of the couches and sat down.

"Now, what is it you wished to discuss?"

I cautiously moved closer and sat down on the couch opposite him. David followed close behind.

"I just had a guy try to shoot me in the head," I stated matter-of-factly.

Raphael sat deeper in the couch with a nasty grin on his face.

"I am little surprised, having so recently experienced first-hand your proficiency at acquiring enemies. But what, pray tell, would you have me do about it?"

I sat there, not sure how to respond.

"This is serious, Raphael," David said. "What do you know about this?"

"Other than what you have just told me, nothing," Raphael sneered.

"Well, do you think, maybe-possibly-perhaps, that you could find something out?" I asked.

"And what exactly would I gain from this venture?"

"Me not kicking you in the scrotum again," I shot back.

David stifled a laugh, while Raphael's expression instantly turned to a frown.

"With motivation like that, I can hardly decline," Raphael mocked.

"Thank you," I said sincerely. He wasn't the most likeable guy, but I knew he'd keep his word.

I proceeded to tell him what little information I knew. Raphael stood up, and if I hadn't been watching him closely, I might not have noticed him wince.

"I trust you do not require me for anything else?" he asked.

I resisted the urge to reply with something witty. He had after all, just agreed to help me.

"No, that's it."

"Then I shall take my leave of you," Raphael said as he walked to the door. I was impressed. He hardly limped at all. Luckily for him he could fly, so he wouldn't have to walk far.

As soon as he left, I slumped down in the couch even more, completely relaxed now that he was gone.

"Thanks," David said as he snuggled closer to me.

"Hey, it gave me an excuse to kick him in the family jewels," I smirked. "That kind of opportunity doesn't present itself all that often."

David hugged me tight as he laughed. "I must admit I rather enjoyed seeing him like that."

"Didn't I tell you I can look out for myself?" I asked before giving him a kiss. "Well, I should head home and try to get some sleep before work tomorrow."

David held onto my hand as I stood up, not wanting to let go of the moment.

"Come back to my place?"

I laughed. "If I did that I'd *really* get no sleep."

"Then care to do lunch tomorrow?" David asked.

"Now that I can do," I replied.

"Come on, I'll give you a lift back to your place."

* * *

The next morning, I cracked open my email as soon as I got to the office. It was usually a relatively painless task to help ease me into the work day. Today, it didn't work out that way. There were multiple emails from the same client, five minutes apart. After working as a computer consultant for more years that I cared to count, I was pretty desensitized to some of the questions clients asked. As long as we were getting paid to make the changes, I didn't mind so much. It's when you had clients that *thought* they knew what they wanted but really didn't and kept changing the specifications on you. Those were the challenging replies, the ones where you had to be firm but not let it turn into a fight.

I had started typing my reply when my phone rang. I had half a mind to finish my train of thought and not answer it, but when I took a quick glance at the caller ID on the phone and saw it was blocked, I had a good idea who it was.

"Dana Harker," I said as I picked up the handset.

"You are at work much earlier than usual, Ms. Harker," Raphael said, his voice dripping with sarcasm.

Raphael pretty much knew every detail of my life, and as much as it irked me, I tried not to let it show. That didn't mean I was always successful, however.

"I take it you found out something?"

"You would be correct in that assessment."

I sat there waiting for him to continue.

"*Aaaand?*" I asked, trying to extract the information from him.

"I suggest that we meet at a more secure location," Raphael replied.

I facepalmed. "You want to see me at the lab, don't you?"

I could practically hear him sneer though the phone. "But of course. How incredibly astute you are."

"It's not intuition, it's knowing how much of an ass you are," I said harshly. He knew I hated going to the lab under any circumstance.

"I trust you can meet me there at your earliest convenience?"

"There's no such thing as an 'earliest convenience' when I'm at work. What time do you want me there?"

"Would 10:30 be acceptable?"

"I guess it'll have to be," I said as I hung up on him.

I tried to get as much done as I could before then but around a quarter after ten I decided to head out.

I had pretty much established that I was friends with Nightcat so if anyone caught me in my feline form jumping out my office window, no one would really take notice. As far as the public was concerned, I knew Nightcat through David and actually hung around with her. Still, I was careful about changing forms in my office. I closed the blinds and shut my door as a precaution before morphing.

I had long since gotten used to the burning sensation as my physiology shifted. The only drawback was that morphing several times in a short period of time would really take its toll on me. Thankfully, I rarely had the need to.

* * *

I wasn't in a huge hurry to get to the lab. In fact, I dreaded going back. No matter how many times I went there, it never got any easier. I harboured too many painful memories from when Raphael had abducted me and experimented on me. I could still feel a twinge of pain whenever I was reminded of that procedure.

I mostly kept to the back alleys, not wanting to draw attention to myself just in case someone else had the same idea of ramming a bullet in my head. I was a few blocks away when my sixth sense warned me of something. It was a dull throbbing so I knew that it was more a minor threat than anything else.

I stopped and had a quick look around when I saw someone in black pajamas about 10 feet away from me. The black hood and cloth around his face implied that he was a ninja or something similar, someone who relied on stealth.

I tried not to laugh at the irony. Here I was part cat with heightened senses and agility, the epitome of stealth and *he* was trying to get the jump on *me*.

"Aren't you guys supposed to be, you know, uber secretive?" I asked.

"What makes you think we aren't?" he replied just at my sixth sense went off in my head like a klaxon. This guy was obviously a diversion.

Several metal objects came whirling at me. I blocked them with my wrist cuffs but when I turned to flee, one stray throwing star embedded itself in my side.

I was getting the feeling that this little episode would work off yesterday's poutine supper. Adrenaline pumping and pushing back pain, I ran the rest of the way to the lab.

Raphael damn well better let me in, and fast, I thought.

Even though the door was cloaked in a holographic brick pattern, I knew where it was. I pounded on the door as hard as I could just as I heard footsteps from all directions. I turned around to face my adversaries and was amazed at the sheer diversity and number of them.

There were several in hunter's apparel, armed with various weapons. Some had shotguns and another a compound bow. And of course my buddies the ninjas were there too. It was like a bad "Village People" re-enactment.

Normally I wouldn't have been that afraid, but I was cornered and instinct was taking over. My mind snapped into survival mode, I let out the loudest roar I could, announcing my presence and attempting in vain to scare off my attackers.

In a blinding flash, a weapon went off, just as the lab door opened to reveal Raphael. He shielded me with his wings, but something still found its way through to my lower leg. Instantly, my calf started to go numb.

Raphael picked up the nearest of my attackers and flung him at the rest of the crowd. He extended his wings fully, tossing the rest of them 20 feet in the air, but not before getting tagged himself. He quickly dragged me into the building and shut the steel door, locking it behind us.

I lay there on the floor, attempting to do a self-diagnostic.

"We should move you to one of the examination rooms," Raphael said as he looked down on me. "Are you able to walk?"

"I have a large object embedded in my torso and my left leg is completely numb. You figure it out," I grumbled.

Raphael shook his head at me as he leaned over to pick me up in his arms. With his augmented strength I knew it wouldn't be a struggle for him. For being so muscle-bound he lifted me up with surprising grace.

I knew he wasn't going to try anything, but I still felt at a disadvantage. I wasn't used to playing the damsel in distress and the whole incident had me on edge.

"How come you're OK? Didn't they tag you too?" I asked.

In response Raphael extended his one wing. Several darts had penetrated through the membrane and out the other side. If the darts were carrying the numbing agent, he wouldn't have received much of it.

Raphael brought me to an examination room that was all too familiar to me. I had spent a lot of time here, none of it pleasant.

Doctor Bertram was at his usual position in front of one of the large consoles. As soon as he saw me, he directed Raphael to the bed in the middle of the room, although it was more like a metal slab.

Raphael laid me down gently as the doctor came over. He didn't even bother asking what happened; he just got to work.

Doctor Bertram was actually the one who had experimented on me and as hard as it was for me to admit, he knew my physiology better than anyone alive. Better even than Trinity Summers, my best friend, who was also a doctor.

"I'm going to do a quick scan to assess your injuries," Bertram replied as he wheeled over some futuristic apparatus.

"This won't hurt," he said as he started up the machine.

"You always say that," I said bitterly.

"Ms. Harker, the good doctor is attempting to help you. I do not think giving him a hard time is the best policy in this endeavour," Raphael scolded as he pulled out the remaining darts from his wing.

Not that I cared much. I was in pain and I was grumpy. Besides, both of them were used to me being difficult with them.

"So what brought all this on?" Bertram asked as he monitored the readouts.

I gave him an edited version of what happened and told him about yesterday's bullet fiasco.

"I'm curious to know how they followed me here, though," I muttered to myself.

"That I can answer," Bertram said as he slid his glasses farther up the bridge of his nose. "It appears that you didn't quite get everything out of the top of your humerus."

"When you're fishing around in your own flesh for a bullet, you sometimes miss the little things," I scoffed.

"Oh, you got the bullet in its entirety, but not the tracking device. It's still embedded in the bone."

Raphael gave him his full attention, but my mind went off like an explosion. Did these people know where I lived or find out about my alter ego? Were my friends and family in danger?

Evidently my rapidly beating heart showed up on the monitor.

"Don't worry, it was glitching," Bertram reassured me. "Whenever you changed back to your human form, it short-circuited the device. It would only have worked while you were in your feline form, and even then only intermittently."

I exhaled in relief.

"The tracking device will be easy to remove. The other objects will require a little more finesse to extract," Bertram said as he shut the scanner off and wheeled it back to its original spot.

"What do you mean?" I inquired.

"Your healing factor is more or less keeping the paralyzing agent in the dart to a minimum. It'll be a bit of a challenge to extract it because of the barbs on the end."

"Then get to it," I said more harshly than intended.

"My, my, are we the impatient one, Ms. Harker," Raphael mused.

"You're not the one with a bunch of pointy things sticking out of you!"

"I think we should remove the tracking device first. I know it's the least painful, but there's no sense letting them know exactly where in the lab you are in case they get ideas," Bertram interrupted.

"Fine," I said as I flopped back onto the metal slab.

"I'll try to freeze the area, but with your healing factor, I can't make any promises."

"I get it," I said.

Bertram went to a locked cabinet for the anaesthetic. As he prepped the needle I had to look away. One of the side effects of the procedure to turn me into Nightcat was that I had developed an irrational fear of needles. It was understandable, but that didn't make it any less annoying.

"You'll feel just a little pinch," Bertram said before stabbing me in the shoulder.

I don't know why he even bothered to warn me. It had to be done and I'd rather be taken by surprise than know the exact moment.

Little by little the immediate area started to dull. It wasn't completely frozen, but it would take the edge off and that's all I cared about.

With the scalpel he made a small incision and then picked up the tweezers. I guess the good thing about having healing powers is that he didn't really have to be all that delicate in the extraction. There really wasn't any worry about making the situation worse or having a long recovery time because of it.

It didn't take Bertram long to fish it out. He handed it to Raphael, who immediately crushed it between his thumb and forefinger and sprinkled the leftover bits into a nearby garbage can. I had assumed they would have wanted to study it or at least see where it originated from to get a clue as to who wanted me dead so badly.

Suddenly there was a loud explosion from the main room. Raphael didn't even say anything to Bertram. He just stormed out of the examination room.

As soon as he left, the noise level increased. My enhanced hearing could pick up quite the commotion outside the room, but

I couldn't discern anything useful. In seconds the noise got more violent.

"Hurry it up, Raphael needs my help!" I tried to rush Bertram.

"Patience, these things take time. And even if I extracted the other items right away, there's no telling how long it'd take your healing factor to repair the damage completely."

"There is one way."

"Such a course of action would be potentially dangerous and reckless," Bertram shook his head.

"Just inject me with adrenaline! It's not like it's the first time you've done it to speed up the healing," I argued.

"And it was no safer back then, either."

I leaned over and grabbed him by the collar. "Do it or I'll break into the drug cabinet and get it myself," I growled.

Bertram, not wanting to risk angering me farther, did as I requested.

"The estimate for a proper dosage is a ballpark figure at best," he warned.

He injected me and I instantly felt the effect. Just like the last time, my heart rate increased exponentially, blood pumping through my veins faster than a car on a racetrack. I started sweating, my fur unable to absorb the moisture. As my body tensed I knew what had to be done. I yanked out the dart and tossed it on the floor. Then I grasped the throwing star in my side and wrenched it from my flesh. I let out a massive lion-like roar to help me cope with the pain.

I could feel my body mending itself, but at what cost? I turned sideways, my feet dangling off the side of the bed while I held the steel frame with my claws and tightened my grip. The metal snapped and I landed on all fours on the ground.

I needed to use this extra energy to my advantage before it wore off. I had to get out there and help Raphael.

I ran on all fours to the main hub of the lab where I found Raphael dealing with the intruders. He grabbed one of them by the throat and threw him at the rest of the group. I could hear bones cracking and snapping under the stress. I didn't like violence as much as the next person, but there was something to be said for self-preservation.

"I had thought you injured," Raphael said as he briefly turned to me before dealing with another onslaught of mercenaries.

"I was," I growled. I really didn't like the effect of the adrenaline. It always made me feel like I was going feral and I very much reacted on instinct.

One camo-clad man ran towards me with a knife. I had a nasty grin on my face as I charged him on all fours, then at the last second, pivoted on my right hand and kicked his legs out from underneath him. As he hit the floor with a loud thud, I thought of a non-violent way of dispatching him.

I picked him up by the neck, ran to the nearest wall and hoisted him up. I slammed his knife through the back of his collar, pinning him upright. I wasn't sure how long he'd stay that way so I decided on another strategy. I snatched the spare knife strapped to his leg and drove it into the wall mere millimetres away from his "daddy parts". At least now he knew I was serious.

As I turned my attention to the rest of the mob, one guy aimed something looking akin to an AK-47 at me. Before he could squeeze the trigger, I launched the grappling hook housed in my wrist cuff and snatched it out of his hands. As the tether recoiled, Raphael easily caught the gun, dumped the magazine, cleared the chamber and easily folded the gun in half, turning it into a piece of abstract art.

Raphael hurled the remnants at its owner, which knocked him over and made him skid along the floor for a good ten feet until he hit a wall so hard that it rendered him unconscious.

"Don't tell me that's all of them?" I said as I looked around. I still had energy to spare, and I was starting to vibrate without expending it.

"I certainly hope so," Raphael grumbled. "I shall dispatch someone to clean up the mess. And repair the main door. Thankfully the hologram projector above the doorway was not damaged, so no one will notice the entrance."

"I guess now you can tell me what you found out?" I asked, still trying to get off the adrenaline high.

"You will surely find this amusing," Raphael grinned.

"Having a dozen people try to kill me in one day is not what I'd call 'amusing'."

"Very well," Raphael said. "Are you aware of a man by the name of Frankie 'The Nose' Costello?"

"No. Should I be?"

Raphael shook his head at me. "Surely, Ms. Harker, if you are to remain in your current line of work you should acquaint yourself with your adversaries."

"I know you, don't I?"

"Adversaries that wish you dead."

"Which you *never* tried to do," I mocked.

"If you persist in this facetiousness, I shall have to rethink my motive for assisting you."

"Fine, what have you found out?"

"Meet me at the Jade River Bridge in half an hour and I shall explain it all."

I raised an eyebrow at him. I wasn't sure what he was getting at, but he definitely had my attention.

"Didn't you ask me *here* to tell me what you found out?" I asked, still marginally confused.

"Surely you would not let your impatience get the best of you?" Raphael chuckled.

"Ugh fine, I'll meet you there," I said resignedly.

"I shall be there shortly," Raphael said as he excused himself.

I headed back to the exam room and found Doctor Bertram peering out from behind a control panel.

"I trust all is well?" he asked.

"Yeah, I'm still a bit fidgety, but otherwise OK," I replied. "Do you have a phone I could use?"

He gave me an odd look, but didn't say anything. He gestured toward one of the large computers.

"Use the keypad there. There's no handset, just speakerphone," he instructed.

"Thanks," I said as my fingers flew over the keys. Even though I had David's number on speed dial on my cell phone, I still remembered what it was.

"Detective Rayner," David answered.

"My, aren't we formal," I laughed.

"Where are you? I don't recognize the number." I knew David recognized my voice but, like Raphael, he didn't mention my name, not knowing whether I was in my feline form or not.

"I'm at the lab," I replied, knowing he wouldn't like the answer.

"Are you all right?"

"I'm fine, David. Don't worry," I said. "Raphael needed to talk to me. I think he's found out something about my 'secret admirer'."

"Oh?"

"I'm supposed to meet him on the Jade River Bridge in a little while. I just wanted to give you a call to let you know I might be a bit late for lunch, but I am coming."

"Be careful. Please?"

"I will, I promise." I'm sure he felt my smile through the phone. "Oh by the way, what do you know of a character called Frankie Costello?"

"The Nose?" David asked.

"Yeah, that guy. What do you know about him?"

"You obviously have no idea who he is, do you?"

"I'm starting to get the feeling that I should," I grimaced.

"He's the mob boss of Grace City."

I tried desperately not to laugh. "I didn't think we *had* a mob in Grace City. I mean, it's not like this is Chicago."

"We still have one, nonetheless. You think The Nose wants you dead?"

"Raphael hinted at it, but I won't know more until I meet him on the bridge."

"Watch your back. I mean it, he's dangerous." I wasn't sure if David was referring to Frankie or Raphael, although I'm sure the warning would have been valid for either.

"I have no plans to die today, I promise," I tried to reassure him. "I'll be by the station shortly."

"See you then," he said just before hanging up.

I wasn't sure exactly when Raphael would meet me there, but I decided to head out. Besides, if I stuck around I'd likely get volunteered to clean up the mess.

* * *

Since discovering it, the Jade River Bridge had quickly become my outdoor sanctuary. The Jade River Bridge, appropriately enough, spanned the Jade River; a relatively small but wide river on the outskirts of Grace City that connected to the upper Rideau Canal. It looked like a smaller version of the Golden Gate Bridge. It wasn't as high as the CN Tower or anything, but on a clear night I could easily see the lights of Ottawa in the distance from the tops of its towers. The bridge gave me a nice view of Grace City and the fresh air was always a welcome scent.

I was sitting atop one of the towers with my legs dangling over the edge when I saw Raphael in the distance, quickly closing in. He had a physical presence that was hard to match. Even though he was still far away I could tell that he was carrying someone by the belt. Under the circumstances I suppose I would have done the same. The man he was carrying had a very sturdy build with a large belly. It didn't take long for Raphael to get close enough for me to see the horrified look on the man's face. He kept screaming French obscenities at Raphael, who simply ignored them.

"If you continue to struggle, I may lose my grip. It would be in your best interest to remain still," I heard Raphael say.

Seconds later Raphael landed a few feet away from me, and dropped the man carelessly on the platform beside us.

"May I introduce Frankie 'The Nose' Costello," Raphael said to me before turning to the man. "I trust you already know who Nightcat is, given that you requested her body to be delivered to you devoid of life?"

Frankie spewed out some laughably ungrammatical French dialogue while pointing to his ear and shaking his head to indicate he didn't understand.

I stared at him in confusion while he continued babbling in French, insulting my and Raphael's intelligence in the mistaken belief that we weren't able to comprehend him.

"Did I understand him correctly?" I asked Raphael in flawless formal Quebec French.

"I believe so," Raphael, surprising me not at all, responded in utterly perfect Parisian French.

"'My tractor is homeless because it refuses to wear a red hat'?" I said in English as I shook my head. "I'm not sure what I find more amusing: the fact that his pronunciation is so poor or that he's insulting our intelligence when we speak better French than he does."

"You see, Mr. Costello," Raphael continued in English. "You are not the only individual to speak multiple languages. We, however, have the decency not to butcher the languages we choose to speak. I believe you meant to say that you can in fact understand every word that we have spoken. Of course, the rest of your little tirade needn't be repeated, much less corrected, in the presence of a 'lady'."

Frankie's eyes widened.

"Now, apologize," Raphael demanded.

"Do you have *any* idea who I am?" Frankie said, attempting to mask his fear and failing.

"I do, and I truly do not care. Now apologize."

Raphael gave him half a second before picking him up by the wrist and dangling him over the river several hundred feet below. I could easily hear Frankie's heart beat faster. He was still trying to hide his terror, but we could see through it quite easily.

"If your hired assassins had not invaded the sanctity of my lab, I would not have become so involved in your little spat with Ms. Nightcat," Raphael growled, showing fangs. "But you have made this a personal matter for me."

"If you kill me, my boys will make sure you become compost," Frankie threatened before turning to me. "You're a superhero, a *Canadian* superhero. You can't just stand there and let him kill me!"

I shrugged my shoulders, knowing there really wasn't much I could do to stop it.

Raphael simply laughed. "I, however, fall into neither of those categories." His expression suddenly changed to utter seriousness. "If you do not apologize to Ms. Nightcat and remove the contract on her life, I shall start at your grandparents and kill each and every person descended from them, including their spouses, starting with your own wife and children. And when your entire bloodline has been properly dispatched, I shall find a most appropriate end for you as well. It is a shame this country abolished capital punishment; otherwise I could simply turn you over to the police and wash my hands of you."

In a single four letter word Frankie expressed his disbelief. In response, Raphael started to recite names and addresses. After the first dozen, Frankie was convinced that Raphael was dead serious. A part of me hoped that Raphael was bluffing, but I knew I wouldn't bet *my* life on it. In the end, neither did Frankie.

"I'm sorry," he squealed.

Raphael was having far too much fun with him. "That did not sound very remorseful. Perhaps you could try again?" he said as his grip loosened.

"ImsorryImsorryImsorry!"

Raphael took a moment before returning him to the relative safety of the platform.

"I trust you have your mobile phone on your person?"

"Yes," Frankie said cautiously.

"And would I be correct in assuming your second-in-command did not participate in the assault on my headquarters?"

Frankie gave him an odd look before replying. "Yeah. What's it to you?" He was obviously trying the tough guy persona again.

"Then he is still among the living." Frankie was visibly shaken by the remark, and Raphael didn't give him a chance to recover. "Call him," Raphael continued, "and inform him them you have had – shall we say – a change of heart?"

Frankie took a moment before reaching into his jacket and fishing out the most recent model of the most expensive cell phone available. He was taking his time doing it, but he also knew Raphael meant business.

"Joe? Yeah, I need you to call off the hit on Nightcat," Frankie said into the phone. "Don't ask why, just do it!"

He ended the call, but before he had the chance to put his phone back in his jacket, Raphael snatched it from him. He closed his hand into a fist and then opened it, sprinkling tiny fragments of circuitry and white plastic into the river below.

"Your cooperation in this matter is much appreciated," Raphael said condescendingly. "I trust you know enough never to cross me again."

"If you don't mind, I do have one question for Frankie though," I said to Raphael before turning to Frankie. "Why did you do it? It's not like I've done anything to you."

He stared at me for a moment until Raphael glared at him. Heeding his warning, Frankie replied, "You're bad for business."

It wasn't an elaborate answer, but it was an answer nonetheless.

"I trust we are finished here?" Raphael asked Frankie, who just nodded.

"Can I talk to you for a minute? Privately?" I asked Raphael.

He was slightly confused by my request.

"I trust that you will remain here?" he said to Frankie. Without waiting for a reply, he launched himself off the side of the bridge and flew to the other tower. I quickly followed him, scampering along the huge suspension cable.

"Was that really necessary?" I confronted him.

Raphael just laughed. "You do not like my methods, Ms. Harker?"

"I never have. That being said, they are effective. Sadly."

"You are no longer a marked woman, yet you do not seem to be overly elated."

"Oh, I'm glad about that part, but did you have to scare the shit out of the guy?" I asked. "Don't you think it was a bit excessive? Oh wait. I forgot who I was talking to."

"If you wish, I can reverse the request," Raphael sneered.

"No, that's fine. I guess I should thank you for saving my ass though," I said resignedly. "And don't think you can dangle me over the bridge to get me to sound more sincere!"

"I appreciate the sentiment, however sincere it was," he said. "I do ask for one thing in return, however."

My heart sank. There was no telling what he'd want me to do.

"Do not make a habit of this. I may not be available the next time," Raphael mocked.

"I don't like it any more than you do," I grumbled.

"Are there any other issues you wish to address?"

"No, I think that's about it."

"Then I shall take my leave of you," Raphael said as he took a step to the edge of the bridge.

I reached out and grabbed his shoulder in an attempt to stop him.

"What am I supposed to do about *him*?" I asked.

"Anything you wish. He is in your custody now," Raphael said before launching himself into the wind.

Great, now he's my problem, I thought.

I hastily made my way back to where Frankie was, but as soon as I got close to him, he backed up as far as he dared, hands outstretched.

"Look, I'm not going to hurt you, despite what you tried to do to me," I said.

Frankie didn't believe me.

"Do you want down or not?"

"Stay away from me, you freak!"

I shook my head. Maybe I was as scary as Raphael. At least I didn't have the amorality to go with it.

"Fine, then you can find you own way down," I said as I jumped off the bridge.

* * *

A few blocks away from the police station I darted into a nearby alleyway, had a good look around and changed back into my human self. There wasn't much sense in going back to the office as Nightcat and then driving to the station. Besides, the Nightcat Express didn't have to worry about city traffic.

As I walked in, I noticed an unfamiliar face sitting at the front desk. Normally the security guards recognized me and buzzed me in, but this time I had to get permission to enter.

"I'm here to see Detective Rayner," I said.

"May I ask who you are?" the guard asked politely.

An evil thought possessed my mind. "There's a birthday party for him in a few minutes and I'm the entertainment," I said with a straight face.

He gave me a confused look as he called up David. After a three second conversation, he hung up the phone.

"He'll be right down."

A few minutes later, David came through the locked door, and was instantly relieved when he saw it was me.

"Happy Birthday," I joked.

"I had an inkling it might be you," David laughed. "I'm glad you're here."

I gave him a hug as I half whispered, "I told you I'd make it."

David gave me a quick kiss before we headed back to his office.

"So, any thoughts as to where you want to go for lunch?" he asked.

"Well, unless you're planning on driving me back to the office, you'll have to pay the tab, so it's really up to you," I half joked. I honestly hadn't even thought of my purse being at the office and how I'd pay for my lunch. Not that it mattered much anyway, we usually took turns paying.

Once we were back at his office, David grabbed his coat. Just as we were heading out again, Sorowski poked his head in the office.

"I just heard something that you may find interesting," he announced.

"Oh?" David asked.

"One of our informants tells me that Frankie Costello just put his mansion on the market and is getting out of town as fast as he can."

I stifled a laugh.

"You wouldn't happen to know anything about that, would you?" Sorowski asked David.

"No, but I imagine Nightcat had something to do with it," he said as he casually pulled me closer for a one armed hug. "I'll make sure to ask her the next time I see her."

"Be sure that you do. I'm curious to know what the answer is," Sorowski said as he left the office, closing the door behind him.

"Dare I ask?" David said to me, with a cheeky grin on his face.

"I didn't do a thing. In fact I didn't have to."

"I guess I should ask what *Raphael* did then," David said in utter seriousness.

"Nothing too bad. At least by his standards." I gave David a hug to try and ease his mood.

"No one died and you're not hurt. I guess I couldn't ask for more than that," David said as he gave me a kiss.

Blood of the Cat

"I'm not sure which scenario is more plausible: you coming here to rescue me or you getting caught while doing so," I grumbled.

"Perhaps I am doing both," Raphael whispered.

"Then what are you waiting for?"

"Patience, Ms. Nightcat, patience. We must first see what this Neanderthal is attempting to do." Somehow, Raphael was the only person I knew that could make something formal like "Ms. Nightcat" sound derogatory.

"You should know me well enough to know patience isn't something I'm famous for," I growled. I was incredibly uncomfortable and I wanted out. "If it helps any, he said he needed my blood for something or other."

"Could you possibly be any more vague?" Raphael chastised.

"Look, he tased the heck out of me and drugged me up with God-knows-what so I'm a bit out of it. He keeps pumping it in the cell. My healing factor is keeping it at bay. Sort of."

I looked over at Raphael and he looked no worse for wear. Not one hair on his head was out of place, not that I should have been overly surprised.

"Why isn't it zapping your strength?" I looked over to Raphael and asked.

He flashed a fang-filled grin. "Perhaps it is because I am more resilient."

I slumped down on the bench. It was one thing to have been kidnapped; it was another thing entirely to be insulted by the very person who made me who - or what - I was today. We both had healing powers, but even so, his body structure was built to take more punishment than mine was. My superior agility and speed weren't much help in this situation.

I closed my eyes and sat there, attempting to remember what the doctor was going on about. It was no easy task when it took every ounce of effort just to remain conscious.

"I urge you to stay awake," Raphael said.

I tuned him out for another moment as I replayed the events in my head. It was like trying to remember a long-forgotten dream.

Not surprisingly, Raphael's patience was wearing thin.

"Regardless what his motives are, we must flee," he said.

For once, I wholeheartedly agreed with him.

"If you think you can break out of here, be my guest," I gestured toward the pane of bullet proof glass.

Raphael quickly turned his head to the right as his enhanced bat-like hearing picked something up. "He is coming."

Raphael didn't need to say anything more. I already knew what that meant: play along.

I closed my eyes and pretended I was asleep. I half expected Raphael's temper to get the best of him and to break his chains and grab the man by the throat when he opened the cell door, but then we would never have found out what he was trying to do. As much as I hated to admit it, Raphael had the right idea.

The door slowly creaked open as the footsteps got closer. The man was mere inches away from my face; I could smell his breath and I had that uneasy feeling someone was watching me.

He patted my cheek, likely trying to get a reaction out of me. Receiving none, he shuffled around a bit. I cracked open my eye just a hair to see if I could make out what he was doing.

He reached in his lab coat and grabbed a needle. My heartbeat instantly doubled. Even with the adrenaline surging, it wasn't enough to negate the effects of the drugs.

I was never a fan of needles, but ever since that fateful day when Raphael had mutated me into a human-cat hybrid, I've been beyond phobic of them. During that procedure he rammed a huge one in my midsection and now the mere sight of a needle made me tense up.

It took every ounce of effort on my part not to react.

"This won't hurt that much. I'm sure you've had worse happen to you," the man muttered and he shoved the needle in my forearm. Seconds later he removed it and didn't bother putting a bandage on. Not that it would have made much sense. It wouldn't have stuck well to the fur.

He gently patted me on the back of the head.

"I can't thank you enough for this. I've been so close for so long and this little bit of information will help me out immensely."

Once I heard his footsteps on the other side of the door, I opened my eyes and turned to Raphael, who sat there with an enormous grimace on his face.

"What?" I asked, knowing Raphael was thinking of something.

"This is most … unfortunate," he muttered under his breath. If it wasn't for my enhanced hearing, I might not have heard him.

"What aren't you telling me?" I growled with as much emphasis as I could.

"That man belongs to a rival organization," Raphael confessed.

"You mean there's more than one of you?" I asked incredulously.

"I surmise that he needed your DNA for an attempt to backwards-engineer the procedure."

"So he can make more hybrids? Wonderful," I said. "And here I thought there was no one else out there as amoral as you. So what's the plan? We can't stay here forever."

"If you would cease conversing, Ms. Nightcat, I could attempt to discover our captor's motive by listening."

Suddenly there was a loud crash and a scream from the other room. Raphael instantly broke free of his restraints and snapped mine in two as though they were pieces of raw spaghetti.

Raphael grabbed my wrist and ran, practically dragging me behind him because I could hardly keep up. He kicked the door off its hinges and we barely caught a glimpse of the half mutated doctor before he fled. Whatever he was experimenting with, it looked like it partially succeeded.

We attempted to go after him, but as soon as we got out the front door and Raphael saw the horde of police cars, he took to the sky.

I barely had enough energy to hold myself up, let alone go after either of them. David quickly ran to my side and helped me off to the sidelines while the rest of the officers went inside the building or tried to track down the doctor.

"Dana, are you OK?" David whispered quietly enough for only me to hear.

"I will be," I said as I shook my head. I still felt like I'd been awakened in the middle of a deep sleep.

"Come on, let's sit down," David said gently as he escorted me to his unmarked police cruiser. He opened the door and helped me in. I sat sideways in the driver's seat and looked over at David.

Being in public with him while I was in my feline form with him was never easy. We always had to be mindful of getting too intimate for fear that someone would figure out there was more to our relationship than meets the eye. Practically everyone knew David was dating Dana Harker, but few knew that this was my secret identity. As far as the public was concerned, I didn't even *have* a secret identity.

"How did you know where I was?" I asked him.

"No one had heard from you in a while so I asked Raphael for help to find you."

That spoke volumes about how close we were. To say that David hated Raphael was a gross understatement.

David gently held my hand but didn't make a show of it. "I'm glad you're all right," he said.

"Same here," I confessed.

A brand new police cruiser pulled up in front of us and our conversation was cut short by Inspector Sorowski's approach.

"I don't suppose you could tell me what happened here, Cat?" he asked gruffly as he slammed his car door behind him.

"I would if I actually knew something," I responded. Sorowski and I rather enjoyed giving each other a hard time.

"And I don't suppose you know what *that* was either?"

"Not really," I half lied. The cover story I used to explain my existence was that I was created from scratch, a human fetus injected with cat DNA. I wasn't about to let Sorowski in on more information that might hint at my true origin.

David gave me a quizzical look; I knew he knew I was embellishing. I was incapable of concealing anything from him. Not only was David a good cop but I was also a horrible liar. Once we had some alone time, I'd tell him what I knew.

"How soon until you're well enough to go after that whatever-the-hell-it-was?" Sorowski asked.

"I wish I knew," I said solemnly. I was wasting time sitting here, but I was in no shape to go after him. It. Whatever.

There was no telling what his abilities might be and I wasn't about to get into a brawl when I wasn't at the top of my game. I only hoped that no one would get hurt while I was taking sick leave.

"You once told me your healing factor was dependant on adrenaline. Why don't you run around the block a couple times?"

I couldn't tell whether Sorowski was joking or not.

"With all due respect, sir ..." David started.

Sorowski uncharacteristically smiled as he gave me a firm pat on the shoulder.

"Look, you've helped us more times than I care to count. We got this. You concentrate on getting back to normal," he said. "Whatever your normal might be."

"If it's all right with you, Inspector, I'd like to take Nightcat back to my place to recover."

"Go ahead. Heal up quick, Cat, in case we need you," Sorowski said over his shoulder as he strode away.

"Hey, Sorowski," I called after him. "Nice wheels."

David chuckled as he watched Sorowski walk away. "He's very proud of it," he said. Then he turned back to me and I knew what he was thinking. It'd be far too risky for him to take me back to my condo or my hideout.

I shifted over to the passenger's seat as he climbed into the driver's side. He closed his door as he started the car.

"You're OK?" he asked gently. No matter how many times I told him I would be, he wasn't going to believe it until I was fully healed.

I smiled in what was probably a vain attempt to quell his concern.

* * *

I admit it felt weird walking in the front door of David's house as Nightcat. Normally if I was in my feline form, I'd use the back door as it was less conspicuous. I was at least able to handle my own weight, but David kept close in case I stumbled.

"That must have been pretty potent stuff," he commented as he escorted me to the living room sofa.

"I feel a lot better than I did an hour ago. I'm not up to peak performance yet, mind you. I'd be about on par with my human self right now."

David sat down next to me and caressed my cheek. Being Nightcat was a double-edged sword. The fur dulled my sense of touch in some respects, but my enhanced senses also let me feel things I normally wouldn't.

I grasped his hand in mine as I looked into his blue eyes. We had only known each other for about a month but it felt a lot longer and people often assumed we'd been together for years.

"Is there anything I can do to help?" he asked gently.

"Not that I can think of. I desperately wanted to go out and find him, but I know if I went now, I'd regret it."

"You've got to learn to shut that sort of thinking down, Dana. Otherwise it'll keep you awake at night," he said softly.

"I don't think anything is going to keep me awake tonight," I said.

"You rest up and in the morning we can both go and look for him."

"I guess. That seems to be the only option, doesn't it?" That fact aside, it was getting pretty late. I should have been in bed a couple of hours ago.

I let out a massive yawn. "There's nothing I'd like more than a hot bath and a good night's sleep." I stood up, ready to head off to bed.

"You should still have some bubble bath left if you want."

I let out a chuckle. "I'm not sure bubble bath would go so well with the fur. Besides, I'm not sure your tub drain would like all that fur."

David stood up and held my hand in his. "Why? Are you shedding?"

"Instead of giving some nasty reply, I'm going to bite my tongue," I replied.

"I could do that too."

"Good night, David," I laughed as I gave him a kiss.

* * *

Another added bonus of me spending the night at David's was that he wasn't near downtown with all the noise. Enhanced hearing, while a valuable asset in battle, was really annoying when you tried to sleep at night.

I got more sleep than I expected and when I rolled over the next morning, David started to stir. I placed my hand on his chest and cuddled him, savouring the moment.

"No word from Sorowski last night?" I asked quietly.

"Nope." David yawned as he turned to face me. "How are you feeling?"

I did a quick self-diagnostic and came to the conclusion I was fully recovered.

"Good," I said as I sat up in bed and stretched.

"I'll make us breakfast then we can head out," David said.

"I think I'm going to change first. I'm all healed up and frankly, I need a break from my feline half. Besides, as good as your cooking is, being in cat mode always makes food taste weird," I half joked.

"Better my cooking than yours!" David said as he scurried out of bed before I could smack him.

I laughed at the comment and let it slide. It was no secret that David was the better cook. I admit I get by, but only just.

I climbed out of bed and changed back to my human form. As painful an experience as it had been to become Nightcat, I at least retained my human identity.

I had long ago became an expert at morphing. I started the change at my fingertips, more out of habit than anything else. The soft brown fur receded into the pores of my human skin, as my jet-black claws lost their colour and shortened into normal human fingernails. The change quickly rippled up my arms to my torso and extended down my legs. My cat-like feet changed to their human equivalents, and I always had to be mindful so I didn't accidentally fall over when I found myself standing on tiptoe. The reddish brown hair on my head shortened by a foot or so and formed itself into my regular hairstyle, although the colour changed only slightly. My pointed ears reverted to their human counterparts, my fangs got smaller until they were no longer pointed, and the amber colour in my pupils was replaced by emerald green. The last thing to undergo the transfiguration was my clothes. Although I could only transform back into the clothes I was wearing before the morph, at least I wasn't left naked. I just had to remember not to be wearing anything embarrassing when I became Nightcat. Of course, anything I owned would offer more coverage than my skimpy black Nightcat costume.

I knew I'd have to change back to Nightcat after breakfast, and I had to watch out not to morph too many times lest I tire myself out. So long as I stayed as Nightcat for a while before morphing back to my human self, I knew I'd be OK.

After a simple but hearty breakfast and a shower, David and I tried to figure out the best way to proceed.

"I never did thank you, you know," I said after a few moments of silence.

"For what?" David was mildly confused.

"For swallowing your pride and asking Raphael for help. I know it wasn't easy for you," I said as I kissed his cheek.

"You know I'd do anything to keep you safe. Even if it means asking for his help."

To this day it still astounded me how I was at least able to tolerate Raphael after everything he put me through, and David was ready to shoot him on sight. David is naturally protective, but even so I find it odd that he wasn't able to let it go.

"Raphael said he knew that guy and that he was part of a rival organization. Unfortunately, that's about all I know, and I can't see it being of much help."

"It's better than nothing," David said. "Rather than wait for Sorowski to call, we should mount our own search. We can start in the area of that makeshift lab. That's as good a place to start as any."

"I really wish we had more to go on," I frowned.

As if on cue, the phone rang. David quickly got up to answer it and while I could only hear his end of the conversation, I knew what it was about.

"Do NOT engage the subject. Nightcat and I are on our way," David said forcefully into the handset.

Before he even turned to me, I had already changed my appearance to that of Nightcat.

"Let's go," I said as I headed to the door.

* * *

David let me out of the car a few blocks away from where the carnage started. I wanted to be up high on the rooftops, but didn't want to expend any energy just getting to the location.

David and several police officers were cautiously surveying the area, guns drawn. Part of my job was to provide overwatch, thanks to the little radio device David lent me so I could keep in contact with him.

The mess on the street was pretty bad. Cars tossed and flipped on their sides, store windows broken and mailboxes tipped over. The only plausible reason for the lack of looting was that people were too scared of the creature. I only hoped that there were no civilians nearby.

I scented the air as much as I could, but I wasn't getting much. I suddenly heard something behind me and quickly turned around in a defensive posture only to find Raphael landing a few feet away.

"I never thought I'd say this, but I'm glad to see you," I said as I stood down. "So why exactly did you bugger off after you rescued me?"

"I do not think the police would have appreciated my help as much as you did," he replied. "The best weapon is knowledge, so I went to my lab to consult with Dr. Bertram and to find out more information about the present situation."

"And?" I really hated when I had to extract information from him.

"The man's name is Dr. Randolph Morhart. He holds the same position with the rival organization that Dr. Bertram holds with ours."

"Evidently he wasn't as competent as Dr. Bertram. Otherwise this guy wouldn't have gone berserk when he mutated himself."

"I was attempting to use an analogy you would be able to comprehend," Raphael mocked.

I looked down at the street below while I continued the conversation. After all, I was supposed to be the lookout.

"So what went wrong?" I asked without looking at him.

"That was the very same question I posed to Dr. Bertram," Raphael replied. "He believes that at least one crucial detail was overlooked. Not only is Dr. Morhart unable to revert to a human state, he has lost all human cognizance."

"Wonderful. Not only is he a man-wolf, he's a crazed man-wolf," I shook my head. "I don't suppose you have any silver bullets around?"

"This is no laughing matter, Ms. Harker," Raphael said sternly.

"Which is precisely why I'm not laughing." I turned the radio back on. "David, looks like we've got a helper. I don't suppose you can make sure Raphael doesn't get shot by one of your guys? At least not until *after* we've taken care of the wolf guy?"

"No promises," he said.

I leaped to the next building to continue my reconnaissance. Raphael flew beside me.

"Not that I'm not grateful, but why *are* you helping?" I asked forcefully.

"Why question providence, Ms. Harker?" Raphael grinned.

He was right. I should leave well enough alone.

"So any idea why a wolf?" I asked as I continued to look down on the streets, not really expecting an answer.

He made a show of helping me look for Morhart as he replied, "This was a rival organization. You are a humanoid feline and in the public eye. So no doubt they chose a canine, or more specifically a wolf, to emphasize that point."

"Don't they realize that a lion could easily kill a wolf?"

"True, but Dr. Morhart possesses something you do not."

He was doing it to me again. "Which is?"

"He is more in touch with his animal aspect."

I looked up at him. "I don't follow."

Raphael stood there and laughed. "I apparently need to spell it out for you. You see, Ms. Harker, when I said that he no longer retains any measurable amount of human cognizance, the point I was attempting to make, in layman's terms, was that he has gone feral."

I stared at Raphael, digesting what he just said.

"And of course there is the added complication of his extremely high metabolism. He must eat in excess simply to remain alive," he said in an afterthought.

"What, pray tell, does he need to eat?" I asked cautiously, as I mocked his speech pattern.

"What does a wolf in the wild naturally eat?" Raphael bent over, his face mere inches away from mine. "Raw meat. That should have been obvious enough even for you."

I stumbled back in shock as my mind ran off on a tangent. In the middle of the city, there was no large prey to hunt. Just humans. The thought sent a cold shiver down my spine.

I quickly turned away from Raphael and spoke loudly into the device. "David, are you getting this?"

"Sadly, yes. We still haven't found much of anything down here other than a significant amount of property damage. Please be careful, Nightcat," David said with concern. "When and if you find him, make sure you come to street level where we can help you. I can't do too much if you're on top of a roof."

"I'll do my best."

The whole scenario had me on edge. It was like watching a horror movie unfold, knowing that any moment the monster would leap out from a dark corner and kill the protagonist – and of course, I saw myself in that role. While being so tense upped my reaction time, I couldn't be so jumpy either.

"I still don't get why you're being nice to me by helping. It's not exactly in your nature," I mocked, as I kept an eye on what David and his team were doing.

Raphael, while amoral, was a man (and I use the term loosely) of his word. If he said he'd help, he would. It was his underlying agenda that had me worried.

"What do you think will happen if the police are able to contain this beast?" He didn't give me a chance to reply. "Standard procedure would dictate they would question him. I do not need him revealing details about his organization or the one I am affiliated with."

I shouldn't have been surprised. Raphael seldom did anything out of the goodness of his own heart. He was far too self-obsessed for that.

I watched as David and several police officers entered the businesses with broken storefronts. No doubt making sure there were no civilians trapped.

"Found anything yet?" I asked David through the mic.

"No, which is good and bad when you think about it. No one's hurt, but he's still out there," David replied.

"I haven't found much of anything up here, either."

I jumped over to the adjacent rooftop when I got the oddest feeling. My sixth sense wasn't going off, but I couldn't shake the feeling I was being watched.

Raphael obviously caught on to my uneasiness and looked around, his senses not as honed as mine.

I sniffed the air to see if I couldn't discern what was making me so uncomfortable. If the werewolf was nearby, he had to be downwind where I couldn't pick up his scent. I had to be extra careful. I wasn't used to being stalked, so I was completely out of my element. At least I had Raphael for backup if it came down to it.

My sixth sense barely had time to register in my head when something large and grey bolted at me. The half man, half wolf hybrid grabbed my shoulders as we did several somersaults before skidding to a halt. He was on top of me and I was straining to hold him back. His elongated snout was snapping mere millimetres away from my face and drooling in anticipation of his next meal. I was at least able to keep him at bay but for how long?

"Nightcat! What's happening?" David screamed in my ear.

"We found him," I replied through gritted teeth.

"I'm sending up the SWAT team! Hang in there!"

"A little help?" I growled at Raphael while stood on the sidelines.

"I thought you preferred to work alone," he mocked.

I growled while I struggled to hold him back, when suddenly my inner cat took over. I let out a massive yowl that could be heard several blocks away and started raking my feet along his belly, claws extended. The best defensive position for a cat is on its back, that way it's free to use all four sets of claws and its teeth. It may have looked like I was getting the worst of it, but I was actually holding my ground.

Morhart hardly took notice of the damage I was doing to him. He was so fixated on killing me it didn't faze him in the least. I could tell he was weakening, but then, so was I.

Unable to hold him off much longer, I mustered all the reserve energy I could and kicked him off of me. He landed several yards away, pieces of his internal organs hanging outside of his stomach cavity.

He lay there, unmoving. While I was grateful that it was over, I didn't like the end result. He may have been a threat, but I couldn't shake the thought that there should have been something we could have done to help him.

"It's OK, David. It's over," I said into my mic. "I'll be down in a bit."

"I am impressed," Raphael ridiculed. "I had no idea you had it in you."

I quickly turned to face him.

"If you're going to offer me help like that again, you might as well stay hanging upside-down in your cave!"

My sixth sense went off and I ducked instinctively. An industrial air conditioning unit flew past my head. I turned to see Morhart, seemingly uninjured, looking for something else to hurl at me.

Raphael, not possessing my heightened agility, got the air conditioner right in the middle of his chest. He struggled to get it off of him, his super strength unable to easily toss the machinery aside because his arms were pinned. I lifted it off with relative ease. It was more awkward than heavy.

My mind was too occupied with helping Raphael to notice Morhart coming at me again. Obviously he had been unable to find another missile, and was going back to the direct approach.

Just like before, he knocked me over and pinned me down but this time his teeth connected with my shoulder, leaving large gashes in their wake. My earpiece fell out and was destroyed in the process as blood spurted from the open wound like a water fountain. It would have been a near fatal injury for a normal human, and while I was sure I'd heal from it, I wasn't sure if that'd be before or after he made me his lunch.

Raphael, repaying the favour he owed me, grabbed Morhart by the throat and threw him into to the brick exterior of the adjacent building.

Raphael leaned over and lent me a hand.

"I don't suppose you have a plan?" I asked as I applied pressure to my neck with my right hand.

"Not as such," Raphael grimaced.

Going into the fight I had assumed it would be easy, having teamed up with Raphael. But Morhart's savage nature and insanely quick healing factor made it one heck of a challenge. The more I thought about it, the more I thought killing him was the only answer. As much as I hated it, I still hoped that it wouldn't come to that.

Morhart had already healed from his encounter with the brick wall. He dropped down on all fours and charged straight toward me. My cat instincts took over again and before I knew it, I was clinging to his back, my claws deeply embedded in his hide. He seemed more annoyed over my tactic than anything else.

Using my own experience as a basis, I knew he'd be faster on all fours. I somehow had to get him to stand up on his back legs, which also gave the added bonus of making him an easier target.

It was marginally risky, but I let go with my hands, trusting the grip of my hind claws, and put him in a choke hold. As I had hoped, he stood up and attempted to shake me off by thrashing around.

That gave Raphael the window he needed to land some well placed punches to our adversary's midsection. Morhart responded by backing up, slamming me into the wall behind us. My claws unwillingly retracted and I slid down his back and fell on the rooftop, unable to move as I braced myself for what would come next.

He pulled his arm back in preparation to strike me, but Raphael was standing right behind him and I knew he had a plan.

I kicked Morhart's leg, hyperextending his knee joint, while Raphael grabbed his outstretched arm and slammed it down on his upper leg. It'd be pretty hard for Morhart's healing factor to work if the two halves of the bones weren't remotely close to each other.

I scampered away while Morhart tried desperately to steady himself on one hand and one leg. He stared at the two of us, growling and foaming at the mouth like he was in the final stages of rabies. His grey fur was matted with blood.

I took aim at Morhart with my wrist cuffs, preparing to launch a grappling hook at him. The idea was that if it was lodged in his torso, his healing factor would only be able to heal around it. I only hoped the idea would buy me more time to figure out how to subdue him without killing him.

"We must end this," Raphael said.

I was going to ask him how, but he suddenly turned around as Morhart, again healed, charged at him. Everything from that point on was in slow motion. Morhart tried once again to claw at him, but Raphael barely got nicked. In response, Raphael wound up and struck Morhart squarely on the jaw. Raphael was close to 500 pounds, seven and a half feet of sheer muscle, and he put everything he had into the blow.

Morhart's head snapped back so hard that it separated from his shoulders. Head and body slammed against the brick wall, rebounded over the edge of the roof, and fell to the street below.

I could hardly believe what I saw. I ran to the edge of the building and looked down to see that Morhart's body had landed on top of Sorowski's brand-new unmarked police cruiser, destroying its roof, shattering all the windows, and making a real mess of the interior. As if to add insult to injury, Morhart's head had landed on the hood, leaving a considerable dent. I watched as it rolled off the car and, as if on cue, came to rest right at Sorowski's feet.

My eyes widened as Sorowski look up at me.

"Caaaaaat!" he yelled as I slowly backed out of his field of vision.

I decided it would be bad luck to cross his path for the next week or so.

"I know you can hear me!" Sorowski hollered, and I knew there was no getting out of it.

"You had better comply with his request, lest you fall out of favour with the police," Raphael mocked.

"You and I aren't finished yet. We still need to talk," I said as I scaled down the side of the building.

Sorowski stood there. I slowly walked toward him, and felt like a child being chastised by a parent.

"Would you kindly tell me what happened?" he said through gritted teeth.

"You know I didn't kill him, that's not the way I work," I said defensively.

"Then who did?" Sorowski demanded.

Raphael took flight as I simply pointed to the sky.

* * *

As soon I got to the office the next day, I received a phone call from David. I instinctively knew it had something to do with yesterday's events.

"Hey, Dana," David said, and I could tell I wasn't going to like what he had to say next. "We have a ... situation. Morhart's body went missing from the morgue early this morning."

We both knew exactly who was behind it.

"Raphael," we said in unison.

Burden of Proof

"I'm afraid I'm going to have to arrest you," David said solemnly.

"Oooook, can I ask why?" I sat there in confusion.

"Well, not you exactly, but rather Nightcat." David barely made eye contact with me when he said it.

I got up out of my chair and walked closer to him.

"What's wrong, David?" I asked. "I mean, I know what's wrong, but why? I haven't done anything illegal as far as I know."

David stood up and gave me a tight squeeze.

"I know you didn't do it ..." he stalled.

"Do what?"

David looked me in the eye as he reached over and grabbed a file folder from his desk and handed it to me.

I sat down on the corner of his desk and thumbed through the contents. There wasn't any write-up, just a lot of crime scene photos of a victim who looked like he'd been mauled to death.

"I still don't get it," I said as I continued to flip through the photos, and thanking the powers that be for gracing me with a strong stomach.

"The slash marks don't look entirely animalistic," David pointed out. "For one thing, there's a thumb. It's like he was mauled by something that had claws like an animal, but hands like a human."

"Like Nightcat," I slumped over in defeat.

"I know you didn't do it," David reassured me. "But it does put me in a difficult position."

I gave him a lopsided smile as I stroked his cheek.

"I know, and whatever happens, I won't take it personally."

David grasped my hand in his.

"But so long as you don't change to Nightcat, there's not much we can do," he pointed out.

"That doesn't exactly solve the problem though."

"No, but you'd be free."

"I'd like to try and find out who, or what, did this. But the only way I can do that is to patrol the city as Nightcat."

"Promise me you won't? Please?" David pleaded. "We have our orders."

"Which are?"

"To bring you in ... dead or alive."

"That's a bit harsh."

David avoided eye contact with me, staring down at the floor instead. As hard as this was for me, I knew it was harder for him.

"They don't want to take any chances," he said quietly. "You have the capacity to be really dangerous and violent."

"Technically speaking, anyone does."

After a moment of silence, he finally looked up at me.

"But they don't have super strength, speed, agility ..." he trailed off.

"It certainly sounds like you guys have already made up your mind as to who attacked that man. So how am I supposed to clear my name?"

"The evidence from the crime scene is still being processed. I'm sure something in there will prove it wasn't you." I wasn't sure if David was saying that to try and ease the situation, or if he truly believed it, but I was betting on the former.

"I can't wait that long." I shook my head. "I know lab reports don't happen overnight and I can't stop being Nightcat for however long it takes them to process the evidence."

"It's OK," David said softly. "The police force has been around a lot longer than you. We can handle it."

It came out a bit wrong but I knew what he was getting at.

"I'm not saying you guys can't do it without me, but you know what would have happened if I wasn't around the day we first met. I can't let that happen to anyone else."

David frowned as I knew he would. I had saved his life that day, and with his older brother having died several years ago while undercover, David knew all too well the risks of being a cop.

"I can't stop being who I am," I said softly. "But I can be more careful and stick to the shadows, that sort of thing."

There was a long pause before David spoke.

"Normally I'd know better than to argue with you, but I can't let you do this." I apparently hadn't convinced him. "You know I'd never hurt you, but I also can't protect you from what someone else may do."

"I can help you, David. I think it's a risk we have to take."

"But *I'm* not willing to take that risk," he gently stroked my cheek. "Please trust me. I promise I'll find the person responsible."

I let out a sigh. I knew it was going to be hard for me, but I couldn't say no to him either.

"OK. But only because it's you asking."

"Thank you." David held me tight, not daring to let go.

After a few minutes, I looked up at him.

"I should be getting back to work," I said. "But, umm, I have a favour to ask."

David pulled back a little and gave me a confused look.

"I came to the police station via the Nightcat Express and my purse is still back at the office ..." I said in a hushed voice, even though it was only the two of us in his office.

David hauled out his wallet and gave me enough bills to cover a cab ride back to NyTech Industries.

"Keep the change," David joked.

"So would this be considered blackmail or extortion?"

"I call it keeping my girlfriend safe," David said as he kissed me.

* * *

Only after I hopped out of the cab did I realize that my company ID badge was also inside my purse, which happened to be locked in my office. A lot of good it did me there. As well as I knew the commissionaires, they still wouldn't let me in the building without it.

After silently cursing to myself for breaking the promise I made not half an hour ago, I ducked into a nearby alleyway. Changing to Nightcat during the day was always a bit of a risk, but one that I sometimes had to take. I couldn't exactly change in a phone booth and not expect anyone to notice. Besides, when was that last time you actually *saw* a phone booth?

After checking to make sure no one was watching, I started to change my appearance to Nightcat. I had long gotten used to the odd sensation of my physiology changing, and while it wasn't comfortable, it was far less painful that it was the first time around.

A few seconds later after my body was fully restructured, I quickly scaled the building to my office window and climbed in. I knew I had to change back, but I was dreading it. One of the downfalls to having a morphing ability was that it took a lot out of me if I did it too often in a short period of time. At least when I changed to Nightcat, the healing factor would take over. Changing back to my human self was far more troublesome.

Against my better judgement, I morphed on the way to the other side of my office and stumbled halfway there, barely catching myself from falling. I lowered myself onto the couch to marshal my strength. Thankfully I had a desk job so I knew it wouldn't take that long to get my energy level up enough to do work.

I lay there quietly until I heard a knock at the door.

"Come in," I bellowed.

As soon as I saw who the visitor was I chastised myself for not asking who it was first.

Victor strode into my office in a manner that was unique to him. It was a cross between a strut and a saunter. He looked down at me but I didn't bother to move.

"Are you unwell, Ms. Harker?" he feigned concern.

"You know full well I don't get sick," I sniped. Victor and I tolerated each other at the best of times. Even though he was the CEO of NyTech Industries, I didn't hesitate to be snarky with him because quite honestly he deserved it, and I was the only one in the office that could get away with it. We may not have known each other a long time, but we had a lot of history.

Victor stood there impassively. I sat up and stared at him, waiting for him to get on with it.

"What do you want?" I asked sharply.

Victor leaned back on my desk, crossed his arms and smiled, or rather sneered; Victor was incapable of smiling.

"I wished to apprise you of the current situation if you had not already heard." Victor was far too happy about all of this. Not that it surprised me any. I was sure the only reason for him coming to my office was to rub it in.

"You're too late, David already told me." I wasn't going to give Victor the satisfaction of seeing my annoyance show.

"I wish to know what you plan to do to rectify the situation."

Victor was one of only two people at the office that knew of my double life.

"You claim to be so smart, I naturally assumed you'd figure it out," I mocked.

"How are you going to manage not changing to your feline self? It would be a terrible tragedy if someone were to fall victim to a crime you could have prevented."

"Not that it's any business of yours, but while David figures out who's trying to frame me, I plan on staying in human form."

Victor chuckled. "I find that incredibly difficult to believe. You are incapable of remaining in your present state indefinitely."

"What part of 'it's only until David finds out who's impersonating me' didn't you get?"

"And I say again, you are incapable of remaining in your present state indefinitely."

I knew what he was getting at. I promptly stood up and attempted to stare him down even though he was a foot taller than me.

Victor casually looked over his shoulder.

"Would you care to explain why your window stands open?"

I stomped over and promptly shut it.

"It was warm in here," I lied. Victor wasn't buying it.

"I must insist that you be careful, Ms. Harker. Should you be incarcerated, I would hate to be the individual responsible for informing your co-workers the details of your absence as well as your little 'secret'," he mocked.

"Don't forget, I know many of yours as well."

There was another knock at the door, so I told the visitor to come in. I was thankful for the interruption anyway.

Darren walked into my office and stopped in his tracks. Victor's physical stature lent itself nicely to making people feel threatened, and he played up on that as much as he could. At six and a half feet, and pushing 270 pounds of pure muscle, it was easy for people to feel intimidated by him.

"I ... I'm sorry. I didn't realize you were in a meeting," Darren stammered. I'm sure he felt like Victor would give him a pink slip just for looking at him wrong.

"It's all right, Darren. Victor was just leaving." I shot him a nasty look.

Victor slowly left my office without saying a word, while staring down at Darren to intimidate him again.

Once alone, Darren returned to his usual demeanour.

"I can't believe you can get away with talking to him like that without getting fired," he shook his head. "What's your secret?"

"He doesn't dare can me so I don't let him bully me. Don't worry, his bark is worse than his bite," I said as I walked over to my Keurig to grab a cup of tea. "Can I get you something?"

Darren laughed. "I'd ask for coffee but a) I doubt you have any and b) if you did, the smell would drive you batty."

"Just for that you're getting decaf." I hated coffee but I always kept some around for clients. I passed the mug over to him and he nodded his thanks.

"So what's up?"

Darren sat down in one of the office chairs before replying.

"I was wondering if you could give a message to Nightcat the next time you see her?"

I slid deeper into the couch while trying to conceal the grin on my face.

"What makes you think I'll see her with everything that's going on?" I asked, as I took a swig of my Earl Grey tea.

Darren wasn't buying it.

"Come on, Dana, I know better," he chuckled. "You two are pretty close and she trusts you. She's going to need all the support she can get."

I couldn't argue that point.

"Could you let her know that I'm rooting for her? I know she didn't do what she's being accused of, and I wish her luck in finding who did it," Darren continued.

"The next time I see her I'll let her know. I'm sure it'll mean a lot to her."

Darren stood up and I was ready to show him to the door, erroneously assuming the conversation was over.

"And can you do me a favour?" he asked.

"Sure."

"Give her a hug for me."

I laughed. "I will."

* * *

I left the office early to attend one last meeting. Usually with office meetings I had some idea how it'd turn out, but this one, not so much.

I parked my car a few blocks away so it wasn't as obvious. I quickly changed to Nightcat and hurried to Inspector Sorowski's office window.

I had run the idea by David beforehand, and while he didn't really care for it, he had gotten Sorowski out of his office for a few minutes. I opened the window and showed myself in. I knew David's thoughts on the issue, but I had to know if Sorowski had my back as well.

I always enjoyed getting a reaction out of Sorowski, and he made it far too easy. I leaned back in his chair with my feet propped up on his desk.

He came into his office a short time later and simply stared at me as he slowly closed the door behind him, as if not to spook me.

I was having a tough time getting a read on him.

"You shouldn't have come here, Cat," he said in his usual gruff manner.

"True, but I needed to know where you stand in all of this," I said as I got up, ready to flee through the window at the earliest sign of trouble.

"You realize that I could arrest you right here and now?"

This wasn't a good sign. I knew Sorowski didn't like me, but I found it hard to believe that he wasn't behind me.

Sorowski slowly manoeuvred over to his desk while I moved in the opposite direction, giving him a wide berth.

He placed his hands on his hips, causing his sports jacket to reveal his police revolver underneath.

"Still," he continued, "there wouldn't be much point in that, would there?"

I stood there in confusion.

"So you're *not* going to arrest me?" I asked.

"If I tried to place you under arrest and you resisted, which you easily could, that'd just be one more thing we'd have to charge you with later on," he said succinctly.

I breathed a sigh of relief, knowing that this time he was trying to get a reaction out of me.

"How bad is it?" I asked.

Sorowski took a moment before answering. "Not all the evidence has been processed, but it doesn't look good for you."

"You know I didn't do it, right?" I had to be sure.

Sorowski let out a half smile I didn't know he was capable of emoting.

"I think it'd be pretty stupid on your part to try and win over the trust of the police department only to throw it away with a crime that didn't have a motive," he said. "It doesn't make any sense."

"Then why does everyone else think I did it?"

"Like I said, the preliminary evidence doesn't look good. And not all crimes have a clear-cut motive. Then there's the fact that not everyone trusts you at the best of times. And on top of all that, you just plain scare some people."

"I suppose," I frowned.

"What makes it more difficult is that the Crown Attorney is so certain it's you, she's just waiting for the evidence to come back as a formality. So officially we aren't looking for any other suspects."

"And unofficially?"

"I'll let you know."

That put a smile on my face.

"Thanks, Sorowski," I said as I headed towards the window.

"And Cat?" I turned back to face him. "This conversation never happened."

"What conversation?" I said, and leaped out the window.

* * *

As the days passed without David finding any evidence to clear my name, I started to feel antsy. I wasn't sure if it was because of that, or due to the fact that I hadn't been Nightcat since then. I had gotten used to being her whenever I wanted, and now I felt, well, like a caged animal.

I let a few more long days and even longer nights pass until eventually I couldn't take it anymore. I hated to break my promise to David, but I had to do something. My freedom could very well depend on it.

I kept to the rooftops and out of sight, only coming to street level when I reached the scene of the crime, which happened to be a poorly lit back alley. Of course, with my feline night vision it wasn't badly lit to me. I did a quick visual survey of the area but didn't come back with anything. This didn't really come as a surprise — the police would have found all the visible evidence already. No, if I was out here risking my life, I had to use my heightened senses, something the police didn't possess.

Nose held high in the air, I sniffed around to see if I could find anything. You'd think after all this time of being Nightcat I'd know that back alleys generally smelled so badly that it overpowered any other scent that happened to be there. Still, I had to try.

I circled around eyeballing the ground when I saw an area that was a bit darker than the rest. I bent over and was able to pick up the scent of blood through the overpowering stench of the alley. This had to have been where that poor man had died. I knew I couldn't linger, but there was something about the atmosphere that changed when I realized that. The alley suddenly seemed darker and more sinister.

I traced the blood scent up the side wall when I came across some fairly light scratches in the brick. I instantly knew what it was. I held my hand up for comparison.

My claws easily could have made deeper gouges, but even with my hand splayed out as far as I could, the span was a little bigger than what I was capable of. I only hoped this was the evidence that I had been looking for.

I stared at the imprint while I tried to figure out how to break the news of what I found and my broken promise to David when suddenly my sixth sense fired off in my head as someone shouted to me. Just as my feet left the ground, I felt the impact and then the sound of two gunshots. Running on adrenaline, I bolted up the side of the wall until I jumped over the parapet and lay down on the roof top. I knew I had to remove the bullet before my body healed, otherwise I'd have to perform some intrusive DIY surgery.

I yanked the one out of my shoulder and tossed it aside, but the one that got me in the back of the pelvis was harder to get hold of. I couldn't see what I was doing, and the stickiness of the blood made it difficult to feel the bullet. The adrenaline high I was on helped push back some of the pain, but I was still in agony.

For the most part I was distracted with the task at hand, but not enough to be unaware of the clinking of footsteps on the fire escape.

"If you know what's good for you, you'll stay back," I openly threatened.

"Dana, it's me," David said as he rushed to my side.

Knowing I was safe, I slumped over, the adrenaline making a hasty retreat.

"Talk to me, Dana!" David shook me.

My eyes fluttered open.

"Thank God!" David said as he held me tight in his arms. I didn't even have to see his face to know he was crying. I could easily smell the tears.

"I am so sorry. I had no idea it was you," he sobbed. "I thought it was the impostor. It wasn't until you bolted up the wall that I realized it was you."

"It's not your fault. I should have told you what I was doing," I murmured.

I tried to sit up, but my right leg wouldn't bend at the hip so David caught me.

"You'll do anything to put your hand on my ass, huh?" I tried to lighten the mood but it didn't work.

"I'm going to call Trinity. She can extract the bullet." David whipped out his cell phone but I caught him before he pressed the first number.

"No." I placed my hand on his cell. "I don't need Trinity to get involved. If she was caught helping out a wanted criminal, she could lose her job and then some. That fact aside, she can't keep 'acquiring' anaesthetic for me either."

David entered another number into his phone before I grabbed it out of his hand.

"I need your help."

"You want to remove it yourself? You can't be serious," David exclaimed.

"Do you still have your pocket knife on you?"

"No, and no," he said adamantly.

"The bullet needs to come out and I can't get it!"

David stared at me and frowned. I wasn't making it any easier for him.

"It's OK," I said as I held his hand tight, in the hope that it would alleviate his guilt. It didn't work.

"What if you changed back and I took you to the hospital?" He was grasping at straws.

"It's not the first time I've had a bullet extracted. I'll be OK." Besides, if I went to the hospital in human form, they'd have to file a report and I'd have a tough time explaining how I got shot.

Even though I'd have a heck of a time removing the bullet, I knew I'd have to be the one to make the first incision. It wasn't the first time I wished my abilities included not feeling pain. The most I could do was attempt to bring myself to a certain state of mind, almost like separating my thoughts from my physical body.

After a minute or so of working up the courage, I thrust my claws into the back of my leg. David held me tight and tried to provide as much support as he was able.

I had a general idea where the bullet was, but I still had to dig around

"I ... can't ... find it," I said through gritted teeth. It was then I heard David reluctantly flick open his pocket knife.

"I'll hold the incision open while you grab it," I said.

David took a deep breath before plunging his knife into me. The burning pain increased and I only hoped it wouldn't be long before he was able to extract it.

David fished around while I tried not to let out a roar. No easy task. After what seemed like forever he was finally able to pull the bullet out and it fell to the ground with a metallic clink.

I started to pass out from the pain. Not that I cared. It meant I wouldn't have to feel that agony and I also knew I was safe in David's arms.

When I woke up some time later, I was in my hideout, with David nowhere to be found. I knew exactly what had happened. He'd taken a great risk bringing me here and didn't want to increase the odds of being seen with me.

* * *

The next morning, I heard a light tapping on my office door.

"Dana, do you have a minute?" Paige asked.

"Sure, come on in," I waved her in my office. As soon as she closed the door behind her, I knew something was up and I could make a pretty good guess what it was.

I got up from my chair and sat on the couch. Paige followed my lead. She avoided eye contact with me so I knew she was apprehensive about something. Paige was normally shy around people, but never me.

"I had an idea about how to help you. But before you say anything, I already talked to David and he's on board," she said defensively.

I knew I wouldn't like what she had to say next.

"I think the best way to catch this person is to set a trap," she continued, "with me as the bait."

I sat there wide-eyed as I digested what Paige just said. Once it finally registered in my head, I replied.

"No way, Paige. It's far too dangerous."

"Not really. You can be there as Nightcat and David will also be there watching over me."

"I can't have you put yourself in the line of fire on my account, and David can't be seen with Nightcat."

"You can stay on the rooftops and out of sight."

"Still, there has to be a better way."

"Not the way I see it. I'd make better bait than you. I mean, look at me," Paige stood up for emphasis.

She was a few inches shorter and smaller than me, but it was more how she carried herself. Paige was a lot more reserved and quiet than I was and her body posture reflected that. In that respect she was right; she looked like the easier victim.

I stood up and placed my hand on her shoulder.

"I appreciate it, Paige ..."

"Come on, Dana. You once risked your life to save me. Why can't I repay the favour?"

I couldn't argue that point. Paige was another one of the guinea pigs at the lab where I was abducted and turned into Nightcat. She had special talents of her own: the ability to sprout wings from her back like an angel. She didn't have the enhanced senses and strength I did in my feline form, but I was able to help her escape. Since then Paige had always felt like she owed me.

"And David's OK with this?" I had to be sure.

"He wants to find this guy as much as you do." That was no surprise to me.

I continued to stare at Paige, knowing I had lost the fight.

After a minute of me not saying anything, Paige smiled at me, dissolving all the built-up tension.

"Don't worry, we'll find him," she said as she gave me a hug.

While I knew she was trying to ease my mind, I couldn't help but wonder "*When?*".

After she left my office I quickly phoned David to sort a few details out.

"Hey Dana. Sorry, I hadn't phoned you sooner ..." he started. "I want to apologize for leaving you at your hideout and not being there when you woke up. Sorowski called and needed to see me right away."

I instantly went into panic mode. "You didn't tell him what happened, did you?"

"Well, not exactly."

My heart skipped a beat as my mind went on a string of endless tangents.

As soon as David laughed, I was instantly relieved. "Are you sitting down?"

I was confused, but answered with a simple "Yes."

"Sorowski actually approached me shortly after you saw him. Don't get me wrong, I would have done everything I could to arrest the guy, but Sorowski has your back, as you put it."

He didn't arrest me back in his office, but I found it hard to believe he'd actively help me. "Sorowski? As in Sorowski Sorowski? *The* Inspector Sorowski?"

"That very one."

I sat there dumbfounded. "Won't the two of you get a slap on the wrist or something from the Chief?"

"I'll worry about that when and if it happens."

"Thanks, David. I appreciate it."

"Just doing my job, ma'am."

As much as I loved the playful banter, I had to get to the point of my call.

"So what were you planning and when?"

"Paige and I pretty much sorted it out. I can't say I like the idea of a civilian being in the middle of it, but I can't really get any of the other officers to help either. Only Sorowski knows that

I'm trying to help you." He proceeded to give me the details I needed. "If you want to stop by on your way home to pick up a headset, that'd be great."

I let out a laugh. "You do remember I have enhanced hearing, right? I don't need a headset."

"You don't, but we'll need the mic to hear you "

After a short conversation, we pretty much ironed out the rest of the plan for that night.

* * *

"Have you seen Dana? It's not like her to be late," David asked Paige.

"I'm right here," I responded into the microphone.

David heard me over his earpiece and looked up, but in the opposite direction.

"I love what you've done with your hair," I joked.

Even from my vantage point several stories up, I could see that David had either coloured his hair or was wearing a brown wig with a matching fake moustache. His association with Nightcat had given him a high profile, so concealing his identity was a bit more challenging than it used to be when he worked undercover.

"Dana, you follow Paige and I'll be about a block behind. We don't want anyone to think something is up."

"No problem."

We got straight to work. Paige walked up and down the dark streets, with me watching from above while David stayed farther back.

I had lost track of how much time passed with us just walking aimlessly.

"Bored yet?" Paige asked in a hushed voice.

"Kind of," I replied. "But if you keep talking to yourself like that, people might think you're a couple of zombies short of an apocalypse."

Paige let out a half grin and continued to walk down the alley. I wasn't tired, but trying to stay alert was challenging. I made a mental note to ask David how he managed when working undercover, although his possessing more patience than I did was likely a key factor.

Suddenly, I heard a commotion in David's direction. Our target hadn't chosen the victim we'd expected.

"David!" I hollered as I bolted towards him.

I found him lying on his back in a shallow puddle. He wiped the blood off his lip as he hollered out to me, "I'm fine. Go get Paige!"

She obviously heard him through the mic.

"Don't worry, I'm on this guy's tail."

I looked up to see Paige's angelic silhouette in the night sky.

"He's heading south on Redland in a blue sedan. I can't make out the licence plate," she said, somehow managing to stay calm during it all.

I climbed up the nearest building as fast as I could, knowing they'd be easier to track from above. I could block his escape if I could get in front of him.

It didn't take me long to overtake him, thanks to my cheetah-like speed. I didn't even need to confirm with Paige I had the right vehicle. His erratic swerving and his speed told me that.

I launched myself off the building, landing about a half a block in front of him and took aim with my wrist cuff. As he sped closer, I launched my grappling hook at his front tire. He tried to swerve out of the way, but only ended up causing a rollover.

My quick reflexes made it seem as if things were in slow motion. I jumped in the air as the vehicle rolled underneath me. As soon as my feet made contact with the ground, I looked back and found the car on a collision course with the nearest wall. Launching my grappling hooks again, I got a good hold of the side of the car and gave it a heavy yank which slowed the car down enough that when it finally did hit the wall, the impact was greatly reduced.

Someone clambered out of the vehicle and I gave chase. Even from a distance I could tell the costume the person was using wasn't exactly high-end. I'd seen better at comic book conventions. What astounded me was that this person was able to pass as me convincingly enough that the cops had a warrant out for my arrest. But I guess from a distance he'd make a passable doppelganger. I shook my head at the thought before taking a couple good leaps to get in front of him. He slammed to a halt and looked around, contemplating his escape options.

"You do realize there isn't much you can do that would hurt me, right?" I said.

His response was to take a swing at me. The burning sensation on my face told me that he had his claws extended. I hadn't exactly been prepared for that.

I grabbed his wrist and slowly forced him to face me.

"OK, that kind of hurt," I said as the wound mended itself. He looked on in sheer astonishment. It's one thing to know about my healing factor, which wasn't exactly a secret, but it was another thing entirely to see it in action and up close.

He tried to turn and flee, but I didn't give him the chance. I shoved him up against the nearest building and raised my arm. He cringed, expecting a blow to the face. Instead, I launched one of my restraints at his left wrist, and another at his neck. The metal embedded itself deep into the brickwork and, try as he might, there was no way he would be able to free himself.

I turned back to see if I couldn't spot the driver of the car, but he obviously had managed to get away.

"Has anyone seen the other guy?" I asked into the mic.

"No, but I'm on my way," David said, slightly out of breath.

"I see someone running down McCormick Avenue, I think it might be him," Paige said.

After a quick second to determine my location, I sped off down the right street. I ran on all fours until I got close. I then launched myself at him, knocking him to the ground. He lay on his back, struggling to get free.

"Like I told your buddy over there, you can try all you want, but you're not getting away," I whispered in his ear.

It didn't stop him from trying, however, and by the time I dragged him to his feet, a flash mob had formed in front of me.

"Kill her!" someone shouted.

Several more joined the chorus, yelling how I was trying to hurt this guy and how the cops wanted me dead. I saw that many of them had armed themselves with whatever was handy. They started coming toward me, all the while I held my prisoner's hands behind him.

"She tried to kill me!" he shouted.

That was all the encouragement the mob needed.

Several of them jumped at me, knocking me over. The driver ran as fast as he could, while I tried to get up without hurting anyone. They had thought of me as a killer and if I fought back, that'd strengthen their belief. I quickly tried to think of a non-violent way to get free of them.

I heard a large swoosh as Paige landed a few feet behind me. She kept her head down, and her hoodie concealed most of her face.

She slowly walked forward as she extended her wings up and out for dramatic effect. I could understand why the crowd edged back. Her wings gave her a truly imposing presence.

"This creature is under my protection. If any harm comes to her, you will answer to me." Normally Paige spoke quietly, but not now. I instantly knew what she was doing. She looked like an angel, so she was going to play the part in an attempt to cow my attackers. I just hoped it worked.

The crowd was silent for a moment before one gutsy person spoke up.

"And why should we believe you?"

"Do *not* question the authority granted to me." To my amazement, Paige actually stared him down.

After a moment of stunned silence, Paige extended her hand, but she wasn't helping me up.

"Rise," she commanded.

The diversion had given me enough time to heal most of my injuries so it didn't take a great deal of effort for me to get to my feet. She grabbed me around my waist and launched herself into the air, the wind from her takeoff knocking back the mob a few steps. Paige gently landed on one of the nearby buildings. There was no way anyone could get us from the street.

"Thanks, Paige. I owe you."

"No problem. Just don't make a habit of it, OK?" she smiled.

I laughed. "I promise."

"You're all right?" she asked in all seriousness.

"I will be. I'm more concerned with David right now," I said as I walked over to the edge of the building and looked down, trying to spot him.

"How are you making out?" I asked him through the radio.

"I'm fine. I hate to ask, but what happened to the driver?"

I hesitated.

"He got away," I said quietly.

"Damn," David uncharacteristically cursed. "Still, we got this guy, so I guess that's better than nothing. Look, I called for backup so you ladies may want to make yourselves scarce. Until we clear this up officially, you'd better keep a low profile."

"Thanks David," I said sincerely. "And I'm sorry he got away," I said solemnly.

"Don't worry about it. Sometimes these things happen. The main thing is we got the other guy."

"I hope it'll be enough to clear my name."

"I'm sure it will," David said, easing my mind.

* * *

After a few days of not hearing anything from David, I took it upon myself to see him in person. I figured he was likely busy wrapping things up. In my usual fashion, I showed up at his window and tapped lightly on it. It immediately opened up as he stepped aside.

"I hadn't heard from you in a few days so I came by ... wait a minute, you're not David," I said as I looked over to see Sorowski flashing a grin at me.

"Very good, Cat. We'll make a detective out of you yet."

Before David even came through his office door, I heard his footsteps and smelled the telltale scent of his signature black coffee.

"Oh hey, Nightcat," David addressed me as he handed Sorowski the other coffee filled cup.

"If I had known you were swinging by, I would have brought you some as well." David sipped his coffee as I involuntarily made a face.

Sorowski took the opportunity to pester me about it.

"Have you ever even tried it?" he mockingly chastised, like a mother would a child.

"Have you seen a cat on a caffeine high before? It's not a pretty sight," I said. "Besides, I make it a point not to consume anything I can't stand the smell of."

David grinned as he slowly took another swig, knowing full well I hated coffee.

"I can smell it on your breath," I said jokingly as I fanned my hand in front of my face.

"Well, it's not like you're planning on kissing me, so I don't see the big deal," he said slyly as Sorowski cut him off.

"OK then, on to more pressing matters ... Cat, I imagine you want to know what's happening?"

"I wouldn't mind. All I know is that there's no longer a warrant for my arrest."

"Obviously there's a trial pending and the whole innocent until proven guilty thing, but it looks like you're in the clear," Sorowski said. "We're still on the lookout for the driver, mind you, because *someone* let him get away."

I stood there combatively. I knew Sorowski was just trying to get a reaction out of me.

"We were at least able to identify him, though," David said as he handed me a printout of the man's rap sheet.

I quickly read it. Curtis Gregory was definitely underling material.

"He and this guy Ron Gregory seem to be pretty close," I commented.

"There's a good reason for that. They're brothers." David handed me another rap sheet.

"And it just so happens that Ron Gregory was your doppelganger," Sorowski explained.

"It still astounds me that you mistook him for me. We're not even the same gender, for starters." I paused for a moment. "The size of the chest should have been a dead giveaway. Only a guy would cross-dress with an F cup."

He must have had to fill it with soccer balls, I shuddered.

"We're still on the lookout for Curtis, but once we find out more, we'll let you know."

After Sorowski left the office, I slinked closer to David. I ran my fingers through his hair with my left hand as I stroked his cheek with my right.

"So, how long am I going to have to put up with you being a brunette?" I asked.

David smiled as he grabbed my wrists in his hands and pulled me closer.

"It's supposed to wash out after a few days, but I rather like it. I might just keep it this way," he kidded.

I hated it enough that extreme measures were called for. "I think the distinguished-looking grey shows up better with the brown," I teased.

I knew he'd be blonde again by tomorrow.

Eye Robot

"So dare I ask how your day went?" David grinned.

"We were pretty busy today with it being Grant's last day. We still haven't hired anyone yet so we'll be short staffed for the next little bit," I replied.

David chuckled. "So in a roundabout way you're telling me you'll be working longer hours?"

"No more than usual. So what about you? Any weirdness happen today?"

"I'm a cop, weird is to be expected," he said as he took a sip of his coffee. "We are still getting reports of UFOs though."

I stifled a laugh. "Ah yes, the aliens."

"UFO is just an acronym for 'Unidentified Flying Object'. It doesn't necessarily mean extraterrestrials," David teased.

He had first mentioned UFOs a week or so ago. The police had started getting vague reports of people seeing small spherical floating devices, mostly outside the windows of high-rise office buildings and apartments. A few times when I was out patrolling as Nightcat I tried to track one down, but came back with nothing. At one point in time, before all this Nightcat business began, I would have been weirded out by reports like that. Now it almost seemed normal. Maybe part of David's demeanour was rubbing off on me.

"I don't suppose we could attempt to talk about something not related to work?" I jokingly challenged.

"Said one workaholic to another," David retorted.

I stared at him for a few moments and honestly couldn't think of anything that wasn't NyTech or Nightcat related. I found myself gazing at his blue eyes and my mind started wandering. I always loved looking at his eyes.

"So what were your plans for the rest of the night?" he asked, bringing me out of my self induced trance.

"Patrolling the city," I teased. "Someone's got to pick up the slack while you're at home sleeping."

David was on the early shift so I knew he'd be heading off to bed early tonight.

"So much for talking about something other than work."

"Workaholic, remember?"

It was fairly early – by my standards anyway – when we finished our supper. I would have loved to stay the night at David's, curled up beside him while we slept, but I also didn't want to get up that early either. As far as I was concerned, the day didn't exist before 5AM.

Normally David would have driven me home, but I didn't mind. After got to his place and sealed our goodbye with a kiss, I quickly changed to Nightcat and was off.

I went to all my usual haunts, but the city was unusually quiet. Not that it was a bad thing at all; it just made for a boring night on my part. Still, the fresh air felt good and it was a nice change of pace.

I scampered along the rooftops when I suddenly got the nagging feeling that I was being watched. My sixth sense normally warned me about danger, but this was something else. I stopped for a bit and had a look around. When I found nothing out of the ordinary, I continued on, though the feeling was still with me.

I turned a few more times to get a look at my surroundings, and try as I might, I couldn't find anything. Then an idea struck me.

I stopped on the rooftop and stood very still. I closed my eyes and tried to focus on any unusual sounds. I had heightened senses, but I still found it easier to concentrate on what I heard if I took the visual information out of the equation.

There was a very faint humming, almost like that of a street lamp. But this was closer than the lights below so I knew that wasn't it.

My sixth sense still wasn't going off so while I knew something was nearby, I wasn't in any danger. At least not at the moment.

I slowly opened my eyes and raised my left arm, using my wrist cuff as a mirror. It was more of a brushed metal look so while the reflected image wasn't the clearest, it would have to do.

The reflection showed a little dark blur. It was hard to judge how far away it was, but the humming told me it was about 20 feet away. Not terribly close, but far enough away not to spook me as it were.

I sidestepped to the right and the blur followed me. I moved forward, and it followed in kind.

I tried another tactic. I ran off to another building, something that had a neighbour with light exterior walls. The hope was that if I could somehow manoeuvre the whatever-it-was in front of it, I'd get a better idea what it was.

It took some fandangling, but I finally got what I wanted. As near as I could tell, it was a robot of sorts. My initial thought was that it was something Raphael sent to spy on me, but then dismissed the idea. Raphael, the humanoid bat who mutated me, already knew everything there was to know about me so there'd be no reason to spy on me. And if there were, he would have been far more discreet than this. For a fleeting moment I entertained the idea of confronting him about it.

Regardless whose robot it was, I couldn't have this thing following me around. The last thing I'd need it to do was follow me to my hideout or worse: my condo. Very few people realized that I even had a secret identity and I wanted to keep it that way.

I raised my right arm behind me, while continuing to look at the reflection in my left wrist cuff. The robot hovered in place. Evidently it only moved away when it thought I was looking at it.

It only took a thought on my part to launch my grappling hook housed in my wristcuff. As I had hoped, the robot didn't move out of the way fast enough. I quickly turned around and reeled it in, sparks sputtering from its damaged exoskeleton.

At first I was careful in case it was weaponized, until I realized if it was, it could have fired on me earlier when I wasn't looking. Once the robot was resting by my feet, I knelt over to have a closer look.

It was teardrop-shaped, with streamlined wings on either side of it. There wasn't much on the shell, except what looked like a lens of some sort. Other than that it was pretty nondescript. Obviously its owner was having it operate more on stealth than brute force, otherwise it wouldn't have been so easy to take down.

I as stood there, I scratched the back of my head. I had "killed" it, so now what? I had half a mind to bring it to David, but he needed his sleep and this was hardly an emergency. Then an idea struck. I couldn't exactly lug this thing home so I decided to take it to the cop shop.

I scooped it up under my arms and headed over to the station. I placed it gently on the roof, near the access door. The robot wasn't going anywhere.

Once I got back home, I texted David to say that I found his UFO and to meet me on the rooftop at 7AM. As much as I loathed getting up that early, I needed to show it to David before I headed into work. I could have stayed up a few more hours, but I wanted to go to bed early, knowing it'd be an early rise. I only hoped I could get to sleep without staring at my ceiling for a couple hours beforehand.

* * *

I met him on the rooftop of the police station the next morning.

"I swear David, I dropped it off here last night," I said as I looked around wildly. "It was broken, it couldn't have just got up and left."

"Maybe it had healing powers like you?" David said, trying to lighten the mood.

I dropped to all fours, trying to get a better idea of what happened. I was looking for anything that would tell me what happened. Skid marks, a scent, anything.

David was right by my side, and when I claimed defeat, I stood up and looked over at him.

"You don't have to try and convince me, you know. I believe you. If you said it happened, it happened. I have no reason to doubt you," he said gently.

Suddenly I heard something far away. I cocked my head to the side and David knew not to ask what I had heard. The sound was rapidly getting closer, and it was very much like the sound the robot made just before I destroyed it.

"David, I think we have a problem," I said cautiously.

"What do you mean?" As he turned around and we were suddenly surrounded by a horde of robots, not too dissimilar to the one I took down yesterday.

Part of me wanted to flee to the safety of the building, but I also knew I had to find out more about these machines.

"You might want to head inside," I said in a hushed voice.

David's finger twitched by his police issue pistol. "There's no way I'm leaving you here alone."

I knew better than to argue with him. He was a highly trained cop, but that didn't stop me from worrying over his safety.

My sixth sense went off in my head like a firecracker. Each of the dozen robots launched a sharpened wire tendril at me and I wasn't fast enough to dodge them all. In an instant, my brain went into overdrive, processing all the pain sensations at once. My feet barely lifted off the roof when the wires suddenly became electrified.

I heard David screaming my name as they flew me to the other end of town.

The robots hovered above a building and while they were nice enough to turn off the current, they spread out, pulling my body taut. Only then did they start to descend, laying me gently on the gravel rooftop.

I knew I would heal from the ordeal, and while the large barbs were still embedded in my body, the most I could do was heal around them. I was going to have to put up with the pain until the tethers were removed.

I didn't even realize I wasn't alone until I heard a man bark out an order to the swarm. He came over and held out a device that looked suspiciously like a large drill.

"The robots still have a lot of juice in them, so if you're thinking about escaping, I'd advise against it."

As he came closer, my heart skipped a beat. I wasn't sure what he was planning on doing, but I really didn't want any more foreign objects embedded in my skin.

He hauled out an ominous looking object from his backpack. It was in the shape of a half circle with flanges on either side, and had a couple sets of large spikes on the underside. He bent over and started securing them over my wrist directly into the rooftop under me.

"Do you honestly think that'll stop me from escaping?" I said with more bravado than I felt.

"I guess we'll find out, now won't we?" he leered.

I lay there in defeat. I was still in pain from the original tethers, but at least there wasn't any electricity this time around. I needed some time anyway to allow my body to heal the best it could.

"So I imagine that was your robot I destroyed yesterday, huh?" I took a not-so-wild guess.

"Do you have any idea how much that was worth?" he growled. "I'll be lucky if I don't lose my job because of it."

So presumably the robot wasn't his, so to speak. I was definitely intrigued.

"Why was it following me?"

"I wanted to make some easy cash. I had access to geographic mapping robots and your little reporter friend needed pictures of you."

Laura Sheeley, I might have known. I swear that woman hated me even before we even met. Still, she wasn't so poor a reporter not to realize I was newsworthy and was no doubt trying to get some dirt on me.

"So I destroyed your robot and now you're exacting revenge on me. You couldn't have been more original than that?"

"I also know the mob would dearly love to get their hands on you and are willing to pay a handsome fee to do so," he sneered.

I heard a faint noise in the sky, similar to the drones, but this was thing was much larger. I started to panic, thinking it was the mob coming to pick up their newest purchase. It didn't take long before I could see a helicopter in the sky with the Grace City

Police Department's logo. It was too far away for the man to notice the emblem, but the unannounced visitor had him on edge.

"Go!" he commanded to the drones. They hastily recoiled their tethers, taking chunks of my skin with it and went after the helicopter.

"This is the Grace City Police Department," David said into the loudspeaker. "Call off your robots and stay where you are."

I was glad to see David come to my rescue, but I was also worried what the drones might do.

They went after the helicopter, the pilot unable to manoeuvre away from them in such close proximity to the other buildings. The robots slammed into the tail end, making the helicopter collide with the neighbouring structure. I knew it was going down. As it spun wildly I could see the pilot desperately trying to regain control.

Regardless how much it was going to hurt, I needed to be free of my restraints. Adrenaline pumping, the animal side of me instantly surfaced. My normally amber eyes quickly changed to green and my pupils were now slit like a cat's. With all my might, I swung my arm up, the spikes embedding themselves into my flesh. Thankfully the force quickly dislodged them and as well as bits of concrete roofing that it was attached to.

I fired off a grappling hook from my wrist cuff and shot it through the tail end of the helicopter. The descent wasn't gentle, but it was a lot better than falling from several stories up. For once I was glad I was secured to the roof. I wouldn't have been sure I could have got enough traction on my own if I wasn't.

I lay there sprawled out, my muscles straining when I heard David down below.

"We're OK," he shouted.

I recoiled the grappling hook and once it was free of the helicopter, I felt the strain on my arm dissipate.

I heard and felt the rumble of the chopper falling over on the rooftop of the other building. I only hoped David and the pilot weren't injured.

"David!" I hollered out.

I could hear him shambling up the fire escape. He was obviously hurt, but alive.

"I'm coming!" he answered back.

I turned to find the robot man quietly making his getaway, as if not to startle me.

"Oh no you don't!" I said as I fired off a restraining device from my wristcuff. It was similar to the restraining device he used on me, but this didn't have any spikes. It just had two pointed ends that embedded themselves into the brick wall with the man's ankle secured between the two.

He instantly bent over and tried to free himself, and a smile spread across my face as I slumped over. No human had ever been able to work any of my restraints free.

I closed my eyes just for a second when I heard David rush to my side.

"Nightcat!" he said as he shook my shoulder. He likely thought the situation was worse than it actually was.

"I'm fine," I said gently. "Well, almost." I glanced over to my other wrist, which was still firmly attached to the roof.

When I looked back at David, I noticed something wrong with his arm. It was dangling limply and he was doing his best to keep it from moving.

Panic rose in my throat. If he got hurt because of me, I'd never forgive myself.

David obviously knew what I was thinking. He smiled as he placed his hand on my cheek.

"It's OK, just a dislocated shoulder. I'll be fine."

"And the pilot?"

"An injured foot, that's all. Now how about we get you out of those restraints?" David looked around to try and find something to pry it off.

"I got it," I said as I ripped the restraints off using my free hand.

"You're OK?"

"I will be," I said as I gave my head a shake. When I looked up, I noticed the swarm of robots were hovering ominously in the air, not 10 feet away from us.

David noticed the panic in my eyes, and before he could ask what was wrong, the robots launched little metallic pellets at us. I pinned him to the roof as I shielded his body with my own. I could tell David was in pain, but I was certain it couldn't compare to what I was feeling.

If the robots fired conventional bullets, I knew I could handle it. These however had something inside the projectiles. I could feel liquid burning its way deep inside my body.

My claws dug deeply into concrete, leaving little divots in their wake. I concentrated on healing and my breathing, but it wasn't enough to stop me from baring my teeth and growling in pain.

"Nightcat?" David winced.

I let out a lion-like roar and I shambled on all fours as I got off of David and faced my adversaries.

The acid was still burning, but my adrenaline was pumped enough that my healing factor was able to repair the damage almost as fast.

"David, get out of here," I said as I heard him reach for his gun. "I'll cover you."

I knew he didn't like the idea of leaving me alone, but he also knew I was in much better shape to take them out.

After a moment's hesitation, David scrambled back to the fire escape. Thankfully the robots were fixated on me and didn't go after him.

I knew from past experience that being on all fours made me a smaller target, but standing up would allow me to have my hands free and to use my grappling hooks.

"Finish her!" the man ordered. Evidently the mob didn't care if I was dead or alive.

The robots started shooting acid filled pellets like mini Gatling guns. I easily blocked them with my wrist cuffs. They ricocheted off and landed on the roof top. A few broke and started eating away at the concrete.

I knew the robots could only hold so much ammo and my plan was to make them waste it. I heard the tell-tale clicking and I knew their reservoirs were empty. A few of them launched tendrils at me, but this time I dodged out of the way and grabbed one in mid air. I yanked the tether as hard as I could, the robot on a direct course to my waiting fist. I hit it dead on and sent the pieces flying into the air.

As much as I hated fighting for my life, at least with robots I wouldn't have to hold back. The situation reminded me of the robots Raphael sent after me to test my then-newfound abilities.

Several more drones launched their tendrils at me. Some I barely dodged, but I remained unscathed. A few had such force behind it that the tendrils embedded themselves deep into the building and the robots struggled to break free.

I grinned as I simultaneously launched both of my grappling hooks. The hooks easily penetrated their outer shells, and after a few sparks and sputters, they landed hard, causing even more damage to themselves.

After crushing the remaining few that appeared to have some life left in them, I went over to the man who was shielding his face with his arms.

As odd as it sounds, I always laugh when people beg for mercy just after they try to murder me.

"You're not going to kill me ... are you?" he stammered.

I bend over to address him. "If you knew anything about me, you'd know that wasn't my style."

He stared at me for a moment and blinked, not saying another word.

"I will need something from you, however," I grinned, openly flashing fangs.

He flinched as I reached down and snagged his cell phone. I stood back up and he relaxed a bit as I dialed the police station.

"This is Nightcat. We've got a helicopter down, and two officers injured, nothing life threatening. We're on the west side of town on top of a building though I'm not sure the address. You'll have to trace the call to get the location."

"We'll send an ambulance right away," dispatch replied.

"You can call back at this number if you need to contact me," I said before hanging up.

I tossed the phone out of the man's reach. I didn't feel like carrying it around with me and even if it was on vibrate I'd hear it anyway if it went off. I quickly headed over to the felled helicopter where David and the pilot were sitting.

"How are you making out?" I asked them.

"Been better," David joked.

"I already phoned dispatch, they're sending someone along with an ambulance. It won't take long."

"Nightcat, I don't think you've met Sergeant Declan Palmer," David introduced us.

"I'm sorry it wasn't under better circumstances," I said he shook my hand. "And I'm sorry about your helicopter."

"Don't worry, she was insured," he said with a smile. I was glad he wasn't mad at me over the crash. It wasn't exactly the first impression I would have liked to make.

I looked down at his leg and noticed the angle of his ankle was off a bit and remembered David saying he injured his foot.

"Hang on, I'll see if I can't put it in a splint for you," I said as I looked around. The only thing I could think of was the wreckage.

I unsheathed my claws and carved out a few small planks from the hull and yanked out some of the internal wiring to hold it together. I didn't have a lot of first aid experience, but Declan walked me through it.

A few minutes later I heard sirens wailing in the distance.

"I'll be back in a minute. I want to make sure they find us," I said to them.

"I should probably go with you. I think Sorowski is going to be a bit upset when he sees all of this," David said as he stood up.

I couldn't argue with him; he was probably right.

"Umm, I have to ask a favour first, though."

I looked at him quizzically.

"Would you mind popping this back in for me?"

I was about to protest, not sure if my strength would cause him more harm than good, but the look in his face made it hard to say no.

Once again David helped me out, but all it took really was a sideways hug. The "Pop" was a pretty good indicator that it was back in.

"Better?"

"Yeah, I'll still be out of commission for a few days, but it's better than it was," David winced.

I climbed down the side of the building slowly, with David on my back. As soon as we got to street level, the officers were just getting out of their cruisers. I hoped that Inspector Sorowski wasn't among them, but I wasn't so lucky.

He slammed the door of an older police cruiser and he stormed over.

"Why does chaos always seem to follow you around?" he asked gruffly. "We're almost through our transportation budget for the year, no thanks to you."

"Sir, with all due respect," David piped up, "it wasn't Nightcat who destroyed the helicopter."

"It better not have been another wolf man." I knew what he was getting at. His brand new police cruiser was practically destroyed during that incident. I don't think he's ever forgiven me for it.

"You can thank me for solving your UFO case later then," I half joked, trying to lighten the mood.

Sorowski stared at me as David brought him up to speed.

"Don't think I'm not grateful, but next time, do you think you could dial back the destruction level just a tad?" Sorowski asked.

Before I could think of a sarcastic reply, another robot dropped into view behind him and powered up. I jumped over Sorowski and launched my grappling hook through it so it couldn't get away. Still in midair, I retracted the grappling hook and hit the robot hard, making a considerable dent in the sidewalk.

Part of the exoskeleton fell away, exposing the inner workings of the device. My sixth sense was going off like a klaxon. I heard Sorowski come up behind me, but I hollered at him to stay back.

Working on pure instinct, I picked it up and threw it into the air as hard as I could. About a hundred feet up, it exploded into tiny fragments that took several seconds to sprinkle to the ground.

"How on earth ...?" Sorowski asked once he was able to find his voice.

"I do know what C4 looks like," I said, even though that was only part of the reason.

I took the time to scour the immediate area for any more robots, but I didn't find any. When I got back, David was just finishing up with Sorowski.

"What's the verdict?" I asked him.

"I'm going to head to the hospital," David said. "It's only a couple blocks away. EMS has their hands full right now, and it's not like my injury is life threatening."

After a few paces, I could see him wince. A trip to the hospital on these rough roads would have been far more painful, but even walking seemed to elicit pain.

With his free arm, he fumbled with his belt, while I stood there confused.

"Can you give me a hand?" he asked.

"This is hardly the time or place," I half joked as I helped him remove his belt. It took me a moment but I knew what he was trying to do. I wrapped it around his neck and placed his injured arm in the makeshift sling.

"Thanks for coming to get me, and I'm really sorry you got hurt because of it."

"You would have done the same for me," he replied.

"And I would have completely healed in a matter of minutes," I said with a frown.

David smiled as he placed his good arm on my shoulder and gave it a squeeze.

"Then you can make it up to me later."

I looked over in confusion and the grin on his face told me he was up to something.

"I need some help with my new work laptop."

At that moment I vowed never to so much as look at another electronic device again–at least not until I got to work.

Case Clothed

The first thing I did after Inspector Sorowski assigned me the case was to go to the hospital and interview the first witness, who also happened to be the victim. There really wasn't much to go on at this point, other than that the victim, Ms. Tonya Clarke, was suffering from chemical burns from an unknown source at an unknown time. All the doctors could tell us was that they were caused by hydrofluoric acid and that the chemical burns on skin don't always show up right away. The incident could have happened a day ago or as little as an hour ago.

"Ms. Clarke?" I knocked gently on the open door of her hospital room. I could hear her quiet weeping. "My name is Detective David Rayner, and I'm with the Grace City Police Department. May I come in?"

She looked over to me, half her face covered in bandages, tears running down her exposed cheek.

I took a step into the room, holding up my police badge as I did. "I'd like to help find who did this to you."

She quickly turned her gaze away, her mind obviously still in shock from the traumatic event.

"May I sit down?" While she didn't explicitly say no, she didn't say yes either. I sat down anyway and took out my notepad and pen.

"I know this is hard, and I appreciate your willingness to see me. Is it all right if I ask you a few questions? You can take all the time you need to answer."

She burst into tears. "No offense, Detective, but do you really know how hard it is for me?"

I said nothing, knowing she was about to say more.

"In an instant, my life has been turned upside down. Yesterday I knew what I wanted in life; now my priorities have changed. And my family lives two provinces away and can't afford to be here with me."

"What can you tell me about what happened?"

"I would if I could, but I don't know!" she sobbed.

"Did anything unusual happen recently? Anything out of the

ordinary?”

“No, not really,” she thought about it for a minute. “I mean there was that stupid freshman prank yesterday, but that was all.”

I jotted it down in my notepad.

“Can you describe what happened for me?”

Tonya grabbed a tissue from the nightstand and wiped the tears away.

“I was walking out of GCU with some friends of mine. The main entrance for the biology wing.” I wasn’t overly familiar with the layout for the Grace City University. I knew I’d have to find out where that wing was located so I could search there after the interview.

“Four guys, I think they were guys, I don’t know, jumped out of nowhere and shot us with water pistols. We all screamed because it was so cold.”

“Can you tell me the names of who was with you?”

She rattled off the names as I wrote them down.

“Were you able to get a good look at the people with the water guns?”

She shook her head. “Not really. They were wearing hoodies and scarves. Most of their faces were covered up.”

I asked for a description of what they were wearing. Tonya told me what she remembered about them and that was about it. There wasn’t much more to the incident other than she woke up this morning and felt like her face was burning.

Before leaving, I reassured Tonya I would do everything I could to find out what happened. I called in the description of the suspects to the communications officers back at headquarters so Patrol could be on the lookout for anyone matching the description, even though it was a bit vague. Comms also gave me the location of the bio wing, though I’d be stopping off at the main office first as a courtesy.

I hopped in my unmarked police and my cell rang as soon as I put the key in the ignition.

“Detective Rayner,” I answered.

There was a laugh on the other line.

"Why do you pick up like that? You have caller ID so I know you know it's me calling." Dana Harker, my girlfriend, was right of course, and I did it more to get a reaction out of her. "I was just giving you a call to see if we were still on for lunch. You mentioned earlier you had a new case."

We had a lunch date planned but when Sorowski gave me the case I had texted Dana that there was a chance I wouldn't be able to make it.

"I'm going to have to take a rain check on that. There's a few things I need to look at and the sooner the better so no more evidence gets compromised."

Dana was always good that way. She was used to my erratic work hours and didn't take it personally when I didn't tell her the details of a case unless I needed help from her alter-ego, Nightcat.

"If you're free we can do dinner tonight instead. Up to you."

"Make it a late dinner and you got yourself a deal. So long as you're not the one cooking." The next morning I couldn't help pestering her. It was a no secret that she lacked cooking skills.

"You'll have to come over to find out," she teased.

We said our goodbyes and I drove to the university. I talked to one of the secretaries at the main office, who offered to take me to the biology wing. She was friendly enough, but I preferred to not have someone looking over my shoulder and asking questions I didn't have answers to. It made it harder to find what I needed, especially if I had no idea what I was looking for.

I took a quick look around when I arrived, but nothing jumped out at me. The stairs were wide and made out of concrete, and the railings were made of the same stone as the walls. A person could easily hide on the ground in the corner beside the stairs.

I walked up on the right side of the stairs, trying not to compromise any evidence that may have remained. I didn't see much other than a few spots of discolouration on the stone wall. I ran police tape around the entrance and at an angle to cordon off the area where the stairs and the building met.

I called it in. "This is Detective Rayner. I need a Forensics unit here as soon as possible."

I searched the area until the Forensics team arrived. I filled them in and they got right to work collecting potential evidence. With the area secured, I could search further away from ground zero.

I came across some commercial sized dumpsters nearby and I had a look inside. At first glance it looked like the regular run-of-the-mill refuse. I put on the gloves I carried in my back pocket and gently moved some of the bags aside to reveal several articles of discarded clothing. Not suspicious by itself, but I knew from long experience that it was the little things that could lead to a conviction. I called Forensics and let them know so they could photograph the evidence and do the rest of the technical stuff they did, much of which was far beyond my pay grade.

If any trace of the acid was found on the clothing, it could certainly be a break in the case. Unfortunately life didn't work like the movies. It'd be a couple of weeks at best before any analysis would be done on it. As much as I disliked police and forensic movies, I found myself envious at the fictional turnaround times. For now I'd jot it down in my notebook, like any other piece of potential evidence I found. At the very least, when forensics was done photographing it, they could tell me the size, colour and make of the clothing. It'd be a start anyway.

* * *

"I'm glad you decided to show up," Dana said as she handed me the box of chow mein.

"I did as much as I could. I'm sort of in the 'hurry up and wait' mode right now," I replied. "I have a few more interviews I can conduct, but until Forensics gets back to me, I don't have that many leads."

It wasn't uncommon for me to talk to Dana about my cases, but I never gave confidential details unless I needed Nightcat's help. It wasn't a trust issue; it was a protocol issue. I trusted Dana completely. I did from the first day I met her, even though she was in her alternate form at the time. I had walked right into a drug deal and they were about to put a bullet in my head when they realized I was a cop. Luckily for me, Nightcat was nearby and took down the crooks before anything bad happened. Admittedly, I wasn't quite sure what to think when I first saw her. Her feline form was surprisingly human, more than I thought would have been possible from someone mutated with cat DNA. Regardless what her form, I loved her just the same.

"You know, if you need any help ..." her voice trailed off and I knew what she was getting at.

I smiled at the gesture, and gave her a kiss on the cheek. "I'll let you know."

She never pressed the issue. She never did. There was this mutual respect between us. Dana had her day job, a computer consultant, and while she was much stronger and faster than me in her feline form, I made a habit of not asking for help unless it was something I couldn't handle. And after being on the force for over a decade, I've seen a lot and can handle most of it.

"Any inkling as to who it *might* be?"

I shook my head. "Not yet. I'd wager that it's someone who knows the victim. It was personal what they did to her. There would have been a lot of hate, or unrequited love, involved."

"And this is exactly what makes you a great cop," she stated.

"It does bug me, though. This poor woman is new to the area, no family around, no one to take care of her when she gets out of the hospital. And she'll likely need reconstructive surgery."

Dana inched her chair closer, wrapped her arm around me and leaned in closer. "You are the only person I know that can remain objective in a case, yet still care for everyone involved. Most times people have to detach themselves emotionally in order to cope with all the stuff you go through."

"Well, I do have a good support system," I leaned over, pressing my temple to hers while I held her hand.

* * *

The next morning when I got to the office, I had already

planned my day; finish interviewing Tanya's classmates, and then chat with Forensics about the dumpster hoodie. I didn't expect them to finish processing any DNA traces on it, but at least a size might narrow the search a bit. Problem was it was a Grace City University hoodie, so quite common. Still, I couldn't dismiss anything without first seeing if it got me any more leads.

I headed back to the university and had a chat with the other witnesses. Their stories differed only slightly, which is what I would suspect if people were telling the truth. If you have a group of people who give exactly the same details, there's a good chance they're all lying.

Before leaving the GCU, I made a quick stop at the main office. It was a shot in the dark, but I asked for a list of the students who purchased that particular GCU hoodie. Luckily for me, they recently rebranded their merchandise so the list of people who owned this new style of clothing was less extensive. The secretary also gave me the name of the supplier: Cal's Custom Stitchery, conveniently located here in town.

It's one of the things I liked about being a cop. When you woke up in the morning you had no idea what the day would have in store. The hoodie list wasn't a smoking gun, but it gave me something to look at. Which was good because I was running out of ideas.

A half hour later I showed up at Cal's Custom Stitchery. They had several locations in town selling novelty t-shirts and the like, but it was their main office that did bulk orders.

I walked in, flashed my badge and asked to see the manager. The employee manning the store took me to the back room and introduced me to Cal. I introduced myself once again.

Cal got up from his desk and waved me to the chair opposite his desk. As he sat down, I could faintly hear the crackling of his joints.

"So what brings you by, Detective?" he asked.

I told him the gist of what happened, omitting the victim's name. For a minute I was afraid the old man would have a heart attack. He leaned back in his chair, obviously digesting what I had just said.

"Who would do such a thing?"

"That's what I'm hoping to find out. What can you tell me about the rebranded GCU hoodies?"

He sat there for a minute, staring far off into space in an attempt to bring the memories forth.

"They asked us to redesign a logo for them. Just a bit different from what they had previously. Most people wouldn't have even noticed the change, quite frankly."

I scribbled down what he had just said.

"How was it different from the original design?" I asked.

"I can print it out for you if you like. Probably better than me trying to describe it." Cal turned to his computer and with a few mouse clicks the printer fired up and spat out an image.

Cal handed it to me. "The one on the left is the original. The one on the right is what we redesigned."

I didn't immediately notice the difference.

"The font was changed slightly," Cal explained. "And the colour was changed a bit. Nothing drastic, but to a graphic designer the change would be as plain as day."

I hauled out the photo of the discarded hoodie.

"What can you tell me about this?" I asked.

Cal put on his reading glasses and studied the image for a moment.

"Now, I can't say for certain because of the difference in lighting, but this certainly looks like the proof that we sent the university." He looked up at me and explained. "Whenever we do a new design for a client, we like to print off a small run, or at least a one-off. It's part of the setup cost. We give it to the client and they can either approve it or not. If they approve it, we go into production. If they don't, we make changes and run off another proof."

"And how many changes did you have to make for this?"

"Just the one."

"Do you require the client to return the proof if it's not to their liking?"

Cal shook his head. "No. We'd have no use for it. Besides, the client already paid for it so there'd be no reason for us to ask for it back. Usually what happens is the client will sell it at a discount to recover some of their cost."

That got the cogs in my head turning.

"And how many proofs do you run off each time?"

"Just the one."

Perfect. If I could figure out who bought it, I could possibly track down the perpetrator.

I stood up. "Thank you for everything. Here's my card if you need to get hold of me." I reached inside my inner jacket pocket and handed him my business card.

And back to the university I went.

The secretary was a bit surprised to see me twice today. I had asked for a printout of all their hoodie sales, including the person who would have bought the proof at the discounted price. She didn't have the information handy but said she could give it to me in the morning, either by fax or email.

When I got to the office the next morning, it was sitting in my inbox. I printed it out and read it before adding it to the case file. At least now I had a name of the hoodie owner: Shane Wilkins. I'd definitely be having a chat with this individual in the very near future.

I headed down to the basement where the forensics lab was and talked to the man in charge of the hoodie, Dr. Kyle Simmons. He had been with our Forensics lab for a couple of years and though my interaction with him was limited, we were on the same page.

"Any time I see one of you cops down here, I know you're wanting an update," he said as he waved me over to one of the desks.

"I know you haven't had it long, but is there anything you can tell me about it? I have a person of interest but I'd like something concrete tying him to the evidence."

"We haven't completed the DNA record yet, but I can tell you the donor is A positive blood type and the hair colour is red."

"That narrows it down a bit."

"This should help you, then. The hair is red, but dyed purple."

That piqued my interest. A positive was one of the more common blood types, red hair made up about 2% of the population, and while unnatural hair dye was more common nowadays, the combination of all the factors was singling out the culprit.

"And the size of the hoodie was XL. Not indicating that the wearer was male, mind you, but it helps with identifying the build of the person."

"Thanks Dr. Simmons," I said as I gave him a friendly handshake. "This will really help."

Back at my desk I did a background check on Mr. Shane Wilkins. It appeared as a child he rather liked conducting science experiments with household items. After one such experiment started a fire in the back yard, Shane's parents were on record as stating that he was trying something he saw on TV and that he was, even at that age, a bit of a chemistry nerd.

I wasn't one for holding someone back from their full potential, but it appeared Shane's parents had found it increasingly difficult to curb his chemical obsession. In recent years, he went from childlike curiosity to attempting to manufacture drugs on a small scale to sell to friends. I had a look at a mug shot from three years ago. He was of average build, a bit on the tall side, with a grommet in each earlobe and a small Chinese tattoo on his neck under his right ear. He struck me as the type who wouldn't hesitate to dye his hair an off colour.

There was a lot of circumstantial evidence around him, but I needed a bit more to make an arrest. But lack of evidence didn't stop me from talking to him.

* * *

Mr. Wilkins lived on campus so I got in my car and drove back to GCU. His room was in the Stanton Wing Residence, not that far from the bio wing. Certainly another piece of circumstantial evidence.

Wilkins was assigned to room 106, on the main floor just a few doors down from the elevator. I could hear a TV going in the room.

I always prefer to knock once before announcing who I was. I've found that announcing myself as a police officer right away will sometimes scare the occupants into doing something stupid, like running or shooting.

After my first knock, I heard someone shuffle to the door. He opened it wide and I saw his purple tipped red hair, red eyes and a reefer in his hand. Once I stated who I was, his eyes widened and he fumbled back in, trying to make a really pathetic escape.

He shuffled backwards on his hands and feet as I walked into the room.

"I didn't do it! Whatever you think I did, I didn't do it!" he pleaded.

I knew he was Shane Wilkins, but I asked him to confirm his name anyway.

"Shane Wilkins, you're under arrest for possession of marijuana." I motioned for him to stand up. When he stumbled, I helped him up and placed the handcuffs on him. I didn't bother cuffing his hands behind his back. It'd look bad if he injured himself while in police custody.

I read him his rights as he stood there, almost in tears. As soon as I mentioned Tonya's name, he immediately got agitated and started screaming at me.

"Mr. Wilkins," I tried to calm him down. "You're already under arrest for possession of illegal drugs. It's best if you cooperate."

It took him a minute, but he eventually heeded my counsel.

"So you obviously know Ms. Clarke?" He nodded slowly as he started crying.

"I loved her," he sobbed. "But she couldn't even remember my name when she saw me."

I wasn't that surprised. More often than not the motive was related to jealousy, money or sex.

Even on the ride back to the station he didn't confess to the crime. But I was more than positive that I got my guy. It was fortunate. His being held in custody gave Forensics more time to identify him as the offender, though I didn't need any more convincing.

* * *

"Ms. Clarke?" I knocked gently on her hospital door.

She glanced over and invited me in.

"I know you mentioned you were having a tough time and how your family was unable to be here to help you through this difficult time ... I hope you don't mind, but I brought along a friend of mine who's offered to help," I said as I waved her in.

"Nightcat?" Tonya was obviously surprised when Dana walked into the room.

"Detective Rayner told me about you, and I wanted to help," she said.

"Not that I'm not grateful, but how?" Tonya was still in disbelief.

"Well, I should let Detective Rayner first tell you the good news."

Tonya glanced over at me.

"I arrested a man last night."

Tonya immediately started weeping.

"Wh ... who?" she managed to squeak out.

"Shane Wilkins."

I knew the name didn't register in Tonya's mind so I showed her the mug shot.

"I know this face ... I mean I've seen him around," she replied. "He did this to me? Why?"

"He had strong feelings for you and was quite upset when his affections weren't returned," I said gently.

I nodded to Dana, who sat on the bed and held Tonya's hand in an effort to comfort her.

"David said things were tight financially for your family, so he and I have decided to raise money to fly them here."

Tonya's sobs turned into streams of tears as she hugged Nightcat tight. "Thank you," she whispered in Nightcat's ear.

"We'll make sure you're cared for and that Shane never does this to anyone else," Nightcat replied.

Being a cop investigating difficult cases was never fun. But at least I could go to bed with the satisfaction of knowing justice prevailed. It made the job worthwhile.

Reconnaissance

"NyTech Industries, Dana Harker speaking," I spoke my standard greeting into the handset. I knew it was one of two people and the unknown number on the call display told me which one it was.

"Ah, I was so hoping I could contact you, Ms. Harker."

"What do you want?" Even if I didn't have a lot of work to catch up on, I wasn't in the mood to put up with Raphael.

"It is a matter of some urgency. Might I see you at the lab?" he asked.

"I don't know. My boss is in a surly mood today, and I'm not sure he'd like me leaving the office when I've got so much to do."

Raphael uncharacteristically let out a sigh. "I am quite certain he would be most accommodating, given the circumstances."

I was hoping to get a rise out of him. No such luck, unfortunately.

"Fine, I can spare some time. I'll leave here in about 5 minutes, is that OK?" I really didn't have the time to spare, but I also knew Raphael wouldn't have phoned me at work if it wasn't urgent.

"I appreciate your understanding and I shall see you momentarily," he said before hanging up.

Thankfully the very nature of my job allowed me to have flexible hours and be away from the office during the day. For the most part, no one really paid attention to my absences and certainly wouldn't link it to my alter ego.

I began my pre-morph ritual of shutting the blinds and closing my office door. I tried not to make a habit of changing to my alter ego at the office, but sometimes the situation called for it.

When I first became Nightcat, changing from one form to the other was a bit of a challenge. Since then I've become an expert on the subject. Unlike fictional superheroes of comic books, I didn't just put on a costume. Instead, the microscopic computers — nanites, Raphael had called them — flowing through my bloodstream allowed me to shift from one persona to the other. I could start the change wherever I wanted, but out of habit I started at my extremities.

My fingernails lengthened to points and changed to black. Fine chocolate-brown fur emerged from the pores of my skin. Metallic wristcuffs formed on my forearms. Simultaneously, my legs underwent a drastic change, converting to the hind legs of a cat, complete with claws and fur. The change rippled up my legs and arms until it reached my torso. I never questioned how, but the nanites were able to convert my clothes to my black Nightcat costume, which resembled a strapless one piece bathing suit with a two inch slit down the middle ending in a diamond shape cutout around my navel. The rest of my body was completely covered in fur, and my spine now sprouted a tail. When the change came to my hair, it simply grew about a foot and changed slightly from its red hue to more of a rust colour. The last thing to transform was my eye colour. Normally emerald green, they were now the amber of a lion's eyes.

My physical stature hadn't changed that much. I was in good physical shape in my human form, and as Nightcat my muscle mass increased only slightly. Still, looks were deceiving. I was much stronger than I appeared.

The lab was a good 30 minutes away by car, but it never took me that long to get there via the Nightcat Express. No waiting for traffic lights and no speed limit.

Generally, my method was jumping from rooftop to rooftop and when they were further apart I used the grappling hooks housed in my wrist cuffs to swing between buildings. Due to my heightened strength and speed, I rarely needed to use that option.

A few minutes later I arrived at the lab. Regardless how many times I went there, I always had a twinge of anxiety. This was the same lab where Raphael had bestowed this "gift" on me without my consent. The images of the experiment flooded my brain and I had to shut it down. Raphael asked for my help; he wasn't going to use me for another one of his experiments. At least that's what I told myself.

The lab didn't have an obvious door. It was a nondescript building and the entrance was cloaked in a holographic brick pattern, blending seamlessly into the exterior. I didn't have to knock; the discreet security cameras would alert Raphael to my presence.

With a sci-fi swoosh, the door opened up to reveal Raphael. The entrance was larger than a regular door, but Raphael still filled it up with his seven and a half foot frame.

"I appreciate your agreeing to meet with me on such short notice," he said as he escorted me farther into the lab.

"I assumed you wouldn't have asked for my help if it was something insignificant."

"You are quite correct," he said as he punched in a security code to one of the doors.

While the lab could be considered a home of sorts to me, I knew it was large and the chances of my not having been in all the rooms was a real possibility. Raphael escorted me over to a large viewscreen that appeared to display security camera footage.

"Our dear Dr. Bertram has gone missing," Raphael stated.

I was astounded. With how locked down the lab was, I found it hard to believe that Dr. Bertram could leave without anyone taking notice.

"I'm not entirely sure what you want me to do," I looked up at him.

"Dr. Bertram is a man of many talents. I was hoping that you could use your computer skills to find any potential anomalies with the security footage."

"You're thinking someone tampered with it?" I asked.

"That is quite correct."

"I have to clear something up here, though. What if he just left? I mean he's not a prisoner or anything. Is he?"

"He is a man with even less of a social life than you, Ms. Harker. His simply 'up and leaving' is utterly uncharacteristic of him."

I didn't know Dr. Bertram as well as Raphael did so I just had to go with what he said.

"You do realize that this isn't exactly within my area of expertise?"

"Perhaps not, but you are the best person for the job, Ms. Harker."

I knew what he was getting at. Raphael couldn't exactly ask any Joe Blow for help. I knew about the lab, knew Dr. Bertram and happened to have a knack for computers.

I sat down at the keyboard and reviewed the last 12 hours' worth of footage at a faster speed. Unfortunately that didn't yield anything. I played around with it for a bit when I finally noticed something small but significant.

Raphael obviously caught on.

"You have found something, Ms. Harker?"

"Maybe." I scrutinized the video a bit more. "There. The time signatures don't match. It looks as though the footage was doctored. No pun intended."

"This is highly uncharacteristic of Dr. Bertram," Raphael mused as he walked to the door, gesturing for me to follow him.

"Where exactly are we going?" I asked once I caught up to him.

"To the good doctor's quarters."

"For what exactly?"

Raphael came to another door, and like before, punched in a security code, causing the door to open.

The room would have been a tight fit even if it was just Raphael alone in the space. It wasn't exactly a jail cell, but there wasn't a whole lot of room. It had a few amenities, bed, dresser, nightstand, computer desk, but that was about it.

"This is where Dr. Bertram lives?" I asked incredulously. I'd seen bachelor apartments bigger than this.

"Not everyone requires as many of life's luxuries as you do, Ms. Harker."

I scoffed. Like he was one to talk.

"So why did you bring me here?"

"I had hoped that you would be able to track the good doctor down."

I facepalmed. "What am I? A bloodhound?"

"Need I remind you that Dr. Bertram is incredibly important to your future wellbeing? If we do not find him, no one will be able to assist you in the future should you require it."

Sadly, I couldn't disagree with him. As much as I hated working with Raphael, he had a point. Plus, I still owed him. He had helped me a few times recently and I hated being in debt to him.

"Fine. Just don't expect me to sniff his dirty underwear or something gross."

My sense of smell was heightened, a lot more than Raphael's and quite possibly more than an average dog. Cats weren't known for their olfactory superiority, but my senses were far greater than the average tabby. Still, the idea of tracking someone by smell was still relatively new to me. I don't exactly keep a mental catalogue of people's scents so if I do have to track someone, I need something with their scent on it so I know what I'm looking for.

There wasn't a laundry basket in the room, and the clean clothes in his dresser wouldn't have had a whole lot of his scent on it. I decided the bedding was probably the best choice.

Man, I hated this part of my job.

After I made note of Dr. Bertram's scent, I turned to Raphael. "Now what?"

"I would have thought the answer would have been obvious enough even to you," he mocked.

"You are coming with me, you realize that, right?" I tried to stare him down even though he was a foot and a half taller than me.

I headed to the main door with Raphael following close behind. Just because I had an acute sense of smell didn't mean I was overly proficient at using it. I was expecting a challenge figuring out which scent was the newest one, but the fact that Bertram never left the lab made it easier — there was really only one scent I could pick up.

I dropped to all fours and tracked it. I normally didn't walk on my hands and feet unless I was running as it was a faster method of travel. Now I just felt silly. It was like a giant man-bat was taking his pet cat hybrid out for a walk off-leash.

Once we started getting to a more populated area of town, I had my doubts.

"You know, if we're going to have to ask someone if they saw Dr. Bertram, it might be easier if we weren't together. I mean, the public is more or less used to seeing me around, but you ..."

I didn't even have to finish my sentence; Raphael knew exactly what I was getting at.

"You do raise a valid point. I shall monitor your whereabouts from the air." And with that, he quickly crouched down, jumped a good 15 feet in the air and deployed his massive bat-like wings.

After about 20 minutes of walking I came to a graveyard. I stood and looked up at Raphael on a nearby building.

"Is something amiss?" Raphael asked as he flew over.

"This is all very odd," I commented.

It wasn't dark out, and even so, I would have been fine due to my enhanced eyesight. But being in a graveyard at any time of day had me on edge. It was very unsettling.

I continued to track the doctor down. The area was much less travelled than the streets so I didn't have to walk on all fours and closer to the ground thankfully.

Moments later I came to a grave marker: Marian Celeste Bertram. The last name couldn't have been coincidental.

There were fresh flowers in the vase. Dr. Bertram had been here.

"At least we're closer," I said to Raphael.

"Perhaps, but it still does not solve the mystery."

I was trying to figure out the rest of the story when an idea popped into my head.

"Hang on, I'll be right back," I said to Raphael as I scampered off to a group of people.

"Excuse me," I said quietly, not really wanting to disturb them.

As soon as they turned around, the colour drained completely from their faces.

I let out a mental sigh. I had thought after all this time people would have stopped reacting to me like that.

"I'm sorry ..."

The one lady pointed and screamed, "DEMON!"

It took me a minute to realize she wasn't referring to me, but Raphael.

"No actually, he's with me ..." I started, but the group fled in terror.

"Great," I muttered. I was hoping to ask them if they saw anyone at Marian's grave.

I trudged back to Raphael.

"Well, that worked," I said sarcastically.

"I would have thought you would have been accustomed to that type of reaction," Raphael stated.

"Don't you start," I threatened as I continued back to the main road. Raphael kept close beside me until I stopped suddenly.

"Is there a problem?" he asked.

"Just 'kinda'," I replied. "I'm assuming he got into a vehicle. His scent ends here."

"Are you not able to track it?" he asked, and I wasn't sure if he was mocking me or not.

"Sure, if I knew which scent was the right one," I spat.

I took a moment to calm myself, taking a nice deep breath. Whether Raphael was giving me some space or waiting me out, I wasn't sure.

"Look, one of the smells is a bit more potent than the other, but I can't guarantee that was the right vehicle. We could be going on a wild goose chase."

"Perhaps, but it is better than sitting idly by and doing nothing," Raphael said in his usual calm manner.

I really hated when he was right.

After about a half hour of following it, we came to the dead end of an alley.

"Wonderful," I stated.

"Patience, Ms. Nightcat, patience," Raphael said.

He paced up and down the alley and I was incredibly confused. After a few minutes of watching him, I ran over and addressed him.

"What exactly are you doing?"

Raphael was obviously on to something and I had just interrupted him.

"Must you question everything?" he chastised. "You are not the only one with gifts, my dear."

It was then I clued in as to what bats were known for. Raphael told me a while back he had the ability to echolocate, but I kept forgetting.

"How is this supposed to help us?"

"Not that I expect you to comprehend, but suffice to say sound waves returning from organic matter and man-made objects differ substantially."

"You're looking for an entrance, aren't you?" I inquired.

"I would if *someone* would cease interrupting me," he glared.

I stood there with my arms crossed like a kid who had just been addressed by their full name.

Several minutes passed before Raphael finally spoke.

"I believe I may have found something," he said.

I walked over to him, took a look and not seeing anything out of the ordinary, commented on it.

"Are you sure your echo location is working properly?" I jibed. "It looks like a wall to me."

Raphael reached out and part of his hand blurred. He had passed it through a hologram. Just like the one at his lab.

A fraction of a second later, I heard a loud discharge and Raphael flat on his back.

I knew the jolt was pretty substantial, but I didn't realize how much until I noticed Raphael wasn't moving. Or breathing.

"Ah, crap," I said as I knelt down beside him and realized his heart had stopped as well. I assumed his healing factor would kick in, but I didn't want to chance it. I raised my fist and nailed him hard on the chest. When that didn't work, I tried a few more times.

"You're going to make me do this, aren't you?" I closed my eyes, brought my face closer to his and mentally prepared myself to resuscitate him.

I was mere millimetres from his face before I felt a hand push me away. I instantly opened my eyes and saw Raphael sitting up.

I breathed a sigh of relief.

He shook his head as if to get his bearings.

"You're welcome," I said as I stood up.

"Do not misinterpret me; while I appreciate your assistance, I am glad I did not require more."

"Me too." I leaned over and helped him up. "I'm betting that Doctor Bertram is in there. I mean, it's not every day you come across a holographic entrance."

"I concur," Raphael replied as he looked about.

He found a dumpster about a block away and dragged it behind him as he shuffled back to the entrance. He could handle the weight of it easily enough, but over time I've learned that super strength doesn't ease the awkwardness of hauling large objects around.

"Did you want a hand?" I asked.

In response he grabbed either side of it, picked it up, twirled around and launched it at the holographic door. It penetrated it without any issues.

As soon as the entrance was breached, a klaxon went off inside.

"I'm thinking someone knows we're here," I said sarcastically. We barely cleared the door before we were surrounded by armed guards.

It seemed to be more of a warning than anything else. My sixth sense wasn't going off at all. And judging by their heartbeats, they were a heck of a lot more scared of us than we were of them. Even so, with that much firepower, I remained cautious.

"Ah, Raphael. So good to see you again," a man in a lab coat and a slight Australian accent came forward and addressed him. He tried to pat Raphael on the chest like they were old friends, but Raphael grabbed his wrist and gently (for him anyway) pressed it backward. The guards levelled their guns at Raphael's head. He let go of the man's wrist and the barrels slowly lowered.

"Aren't you going to introduce us?" I asked Raphael with more than a hint of sarcasm in my voice.

"Perhaps, if he possessed greater social stature than a gnat," Raphael shot back.

"You may have forgotten your manners, but I certainly haven't." The man stepped forward and extended his hand.

I glanced over at Raphael. His expression wasn't warning me of anything, nor was my sixth sense going off. I firmly shook it as he said, "Dr. Ian Hastings. And you are Nightcat, I presume?"

I didn't bother responding. It was obvious he knew who I was and was just feigning politeness.

"And here I thought you didn't play well with others," he quipped to Raphael. "Though I can see why you made an exception for her. I never thought I'd ever see you whipped."

I could hear Raphael let out a low growl, inaudible to human ears.

I placed my hand on his shoulder in a futile attempt to stop him.

"We came for Bertram," I whispered, trying to regain Raphael's focus.

"Having him in our custody was our original goal, but having the two of you here is a nice added bonus," Hastings replied.

"So you do have him?" I had to be sure.

He grinned at me as he grabbed a device from his pocket and pressed a button. In the back of the room, a large metal door rose, revealing steel bars on the other side, with Dr. Bertram beyond them.

In that split second, instinct took over. As I leaped over the guards' heads, Raphael ducked and swung his massive tail around, knocking the guards flat on their backs. I somersaulted in mid air and scampered on all fours towards the cage. I heard a pop in the air like a pellet gun and a slight burning sensation in my arm, but I ignored it. The door was descending back into place. Hastings had obviously hit the switch again. I stood up and caught the door in my hands, my super strength allowing me to keep the door from shutting completely. Still, I was only mortal, and was feeling the strain on my whole body. I extended the claws on my feet in an attempt to gain traction.

"I can't hold it much longer!" I looked over at Raphael who charged Dr. Hastings and grabbed him by the throat, lifting him well off the ground. Raphael pressed the button and then crushed the device.

The door receded into the ceiling. At least that was one less thing to worry about.

"Raphael!" I hollered as I launched a restraining device out of my wrist cuff. He easily caught it in mid-air and, as I had hoped, used it to pin the doctor to the wall.

"Are you OK?" I asked Bertram.

He looked up at me, pain filling his eyes.

"Hang on, I'll get you out of here." I grabbed a bar in each hand and heaved. They were made out of heavy steel, but I was still able to bend them enough to gain access to the interior of the cell.

Bertram was chained to the wall and hung limply from them. They obviously had been after his knowledge, not his loyalty, and he hadn't cooperated.

With one quick swipe of my claws, I made short work of his shackles and caught him before he slumped to the ground.

"We must hurry, lest they request backup," Raphael said.

"I wouldn't be in such a hurry to leave," Hastings chuckled. Each of you has been tagged with a proximity sensor and a bomb. The only way any of you are leaving the lab is in tiny little chunks."

"It's true," Dr. Bertram muttered. "But there should be a way to deactivate them."

Raphael walked over to one of the large computers and grabbed a few more chairs at a nearby station. I picked Bertram up in my arms and walked over and gently sat him down on the chair, making sure he had enough strength to support his own weight.

Even though he wasn't in full health, his fingers still flew over the keyboard at their usual rate. I was curious what Bertram would be able to do, given he wouldn't have had access to these computers.

"I'm trying to log in remotely to our computers at the lab," he stated. "With a sufficiently sophisticated computer and the correct login credentials, it should possible to access them."

A few seconds later, he got past the login screen. That was only part of the battle. I wasn't a stranger to computers, but I could only make out part of what he was doing. I didn't believe Dr. Bertram was a hacker; he just knew the system that well.

A few more intense minutes went by before he claimed victory.

"They're deactivated now, but I still think we should remove the foreign objects from our bodies as a precaution."

I couldn't have agreed more, though I didn't much care what he was implying.

I unsheathed a claw and plunged it deep into my skin. No matter how many times I've had to extract shrapnel from my tissue, it never got any easier or less painful. With a one giant breath, I yanked it out, my body healing almost instantly.

When I looked over, Raphael was doing the same, though he didn't let on that there was any more pain than a paper cut.

Bertram ran his fingers along the keypad and a compartment next to the monitor opened up to reveal a vial and syringe, along with a scalpel and a few other surgical instruments. He quickly injected himself with what I assumed was a local anaesthetic and removed the object once the freezing took effect. I expected him to sew up the incision, but he grabbed a small vial of glue and dabbed it on his skin after pressing the incision closed.

"How do we know for sure it worked and that we got it all out?" I asked.

Without saying a word Raphael grabbed the devices and walked over to Dr. Hastings. He forced Hastings' mouth open, shoved them down his throat, then forced his mouth closed. With one quick tug he ripped my restraint from the doctor's neck, carried him to the door, and tossed him through it.

I knew what Raphael was like, but I was still surprised at what he had just done.

The doctor lay on the other side of the threshold, unmoving but still in one piece.
"I guess that answers that question."
Raphael gestured towards the door. "Shall we be off?"

Emergence

For 20 years and counting, the citizens of Grace City have gotten used to seeing one crime-fighting cat hybrid. What they don't realize is that there are now two ... and that I'm Nightcat's daughter.

"Come on, throw your best punch."

An idea formed in my head as a smirk emerged on my face.

Attempting to take my opponent by surprise, I skillfully executed a roundhouse kick. Unfortunately, my plan didn't work as I had hoped.

She caught my foot in midair and threw me to the ground. As I lay there on my back she advanced on me.

"That was a funny looking punch," she said as she extended her hand.

Not learning my lesson the first time around, I reached out, grabbed her hand and, using my super strength, tried to pull her towards me and off balance. That didn't work either.

"Nice try. You *almost* had me that time."

I stood up and dusted myself off.

"You're just being nice because you're my mom," I muttered.

"Most daughters would accuse their parents of being too hard on them," Mom laughed. "Seriously though, I am seeing an improvement. Your reaction time is quicker, you're better at thinking on your feet ..."

"Again you're humouring me. I don't know why we have to do all this training. I inherited all your cat-like abilities and it's not like anyone in this city could really hurt me."

Mom let out a sigh as she sat down on the edge of the building and waved me over.

"Sarah, you know why," she said gently as I sat down beside her. "We're lucky we're even doing this much."

She was right, I did know. But it didn't stop me from protesting.

The day I found out who Mom really was and discovered that she had passed her abilities to me, Dad was worried. Not about the me-being-a-cat-hybrid thing, but the afraid-I'd-want-to-follow in-my-mother's-pawprints-and-fight-crime thing. It was only through extensive persuasion that Mom finally convinced Dad. With one requirement: she would train me on a trial basis. Dad wasn't usually this overprotective, but these were different circumstances. Besides, he knew what I was like - it was either Mom trained me or I went and figured it out on my own. No one was going to stop me from learning more about this side of me.

Ever since I could remember, I had this incredible fascination with Nightcat. As I got older I figured it was no different than kids liking fictional comic book superheroes. Now that I look back on it, the connection was likely genetic. Don't get me wrong, Mom and I still had our disagreements, but we didn't hate each other. I didn't mind spending time with her. Especially now.

"So, how come Dad doesn't worry about you?" I asked.

"Oh, don't kid yourself, he does."

I looked up at her. "But he doesn't stop you from going out as Nightcat."

"He knows better," she laughed. "Nightcat is a part of me, and has been for a very long time. I can't stop being her any more than you can stop being Nightfall."

"Are you going to retire once I'm ready to go solo?"

I remembered the argument my parents had the day I first changed.   Dad suggested that Mom was unknowingly encouraging me by still going out in her alternate form.

"I wasn't planning on it."

"But Dad said your healing factor ..."

"... isn't what it used to be. That's true, but it's not like it's gone. I don't heal as fast as I used to, but I still heal pretty quickly."

Mom gave my hand a little squeeze.

"And you're not afraid?" I asked.

"I'd be lying if I said I was *never* afraid. That being said, the less I get injured, the less I have to worry about how fast I can heal. There will always be some degree of fear, but you have to be confident in your abilities. Know your limits but always test them."

We sat there in silence for a minute or two. There was still so much I wanted to know about Mom's alter ego.

"Can I ask you something?"

"Always," Mom smiled at me.

"You told me that I had to keep this a secret, right? So why do so many people know about you?"

She knew exactly what I was getting at. More than a half dozen people knew about my mother's secret.

"Honestly, a lot of them found out by accident."

"And Dad?"

"Him too," she laughed.

"Really? I figured he'd be the first you would have told."

"Keep in mind that I'd only just met your father a day after becoming Nightcat."

"And if he didn't find out accidentally, when would you have told him?"

Mom knew exactly what I was up to. I could tell by the look on her face, and like her, I was a terrible liar.

"I know what you're getting at, Sarah," she mockingly scolded me. "We can discuss it when the time comes. For now, it's best not to tell anyone."

I protested. "But this is *my* secret."

Mom was used to dealing with my stubbornness and handled it in stride.

"If it were just about you, then I wouldn't mind so much. But if you tell someone who you really are, they will figure out my secret, and quite possibly your brother's. Sharing this doesn't just affect you; it affects our whole family."

"It's not like the city has any big time criminals in it anymore, so who cares if people know? No one is going to come after us." I wasn't trying to be rude, just making a point.

"Please Sarah, do as I ask."

I didn't have to like it, but I would do as she asked. I didn't think it was fair having her decide who I could share this with. I mean, it is a pretty big deal. I was going through a life-changing event and I couldn't even share it with my best friend.

She gave me a firm hug, and while it helped a little, I was still a bit bummed.

"I can't say I know exactly what you're going through because I don't. This was forced on me and in the beginning, after the change, I really didn't want it. I wasn't excited to have it like you are."

I scoffed. "How couldn't you? You're what every kid dreams of being."

"Perhaps the end result. What most people don't realize is just how much pain there was. I still get nightmares about it."

I hugged her back tightly. I was curious about the details of how Nightcat came to be, but I wasn't going to press the issue. My curiosity could wait for another time.

"Thanks for all of this," I said sincerely.

"You know I'd do anything for you." I looked at her and grinned. "Except that. You don't need a new iPhone. Yours works just fine."

I couldn't resist giving her a hard time. If I didn't, Mom would likely think something was up.

We sat there enjoying each other's company without the complication of words. I stared at the street below, the vehicle headlights reflecting off the damp roads. One by one, the street lights were starting to turn on. Not that I needed the extra light. I was discovering just how much my eyesight and night vision had improved. I could even make out facial features of the people sitting by the window in the diner a block away.

A spark of recognition went off in my head. Not believing what my eyes told me, I did a double blink but it was still the same. I *knew* those people. We went to school together. Robbie Peterson was a friend of mine (hopefully more someday), and he was sitting next to Amanda Carpenter. Saying she was my arch rival would have been wrong. She hardly knew I existed. She was far too busy being the popular snooty cheerleader. Robbie had decent taste so why he'd be seen with her was beyond me.

I knew how to find out.

"Umm, I just remembered I had some homework I need to finish for tomorrow," I said as I stood up.

Mom gave me an odd look. If she thought something was up, she didn't mention it.

"Sarah, that was part of the deal. You were to have your homework finished before we went out."

"I know Mom, I know. And I'm sorry, it just slipped my mind." I hated having to ditch her, but I knew she wouldn't approve of me spying on people. With or without the super powers.

"We can continue this tomorrow night. After *all* your homework is done," Mom said.

"Cross my heart."

* * *

It didn't take long to get home and sneak back out. Mom had changed back into her human form, and without her enhanced hearing I was sure she wouldn't catch me on the way out.

I went back to the same building Mom and I trained on. It was a good vantage point and Robbie and Amanda were still at the diner. It didn't look like much was going on. There was the occasional awkward smile, but that was about it. Maybe it was their first date?

In typical cat fashion, I let my curiosity get the better of me. I jumped to the next rooftop, then the next. I was on the building across the street from them when I saw them get up and pay their bill. I could make out parts of the conversation. Amanda thanked Robbie, he said "You're welcome", and that was about it.

They left the diner, and she gave him a hug before heading the other direction to the nearest bus stop. He waved to her and she waved back. It all seemed very weird to me. There wasn't an ounce of chemistry between them. The whole thing looked staged.

Robbie waited for a minute before putting his earphones in and turning his MP3 player on. From where I stood I could easily hear what he was listening to. I let out a silent giggle because that particular song was also on my iPhone. He might not have the greatest taste in girlfriends, but he did when it came to music.

While my hearing was enhanced, I could tell that he had the music up pretty loud. I was still watching over him when I saw someone bundled up in a hoodie come out of the alley behind him. It wasn't what he was wearing that had me concerned, but how he was acting – head down, hoodie covering up his face, hands in his pockets ... he was trying to look casual yet looked anything but.

Even with my enhanced reflexes, I wasn't quite fast enough. I was still across the street when he swiped Robbie's MP3 player. Hoodie guy pushed Robbie to the ground and ran off, but Robbie didn't appear hurt. Still, I couldn't let him get away with what he'd done. Even before all this cat business, Mom had instilled in me a sense of responsibility.

I scampered down the building as quickly as I could and ran to catch up to the mugger. I was disappointed the chase didn't last longer.

As soon as he saw me standing in front of him, he darted off to a nearby alley. I strolled around the corner, his rapidly beating heart and heavy breathing giving him away. I was trying to be quiet too, although I wasn't worried about giving myself away. Hoodie guy already knew I was coming for him.

I smiled at the thought. Not only could I hear him, but I could *smell* him. I never before realized how much humans rely on sight and sound on a daily basis. It was sad that such experiences were lost because the other senses were generally overlooked.

I walked closer to the dumpster, hearing his heart beating faster with every step I took toward him. Step, *thump*. Step, *thump*. He must have been looking under the dumpster at my feet to see how close I was, because I was sure he couldn't hear me.

Suddenly, my brain started tingling so much it was almost like a headache. I immediately knew what it was - my sixth sense. It didn't go off when I sparred with my mother so the feeling was new for me. Instinctively, I moved out of the way as a wooden pallet sailed through the air. It flew past me, struck the ground on its corner and fell over.

The man only had time to run about three steps before I ripped a piece off the pallet and threw it at his feet, tripping him. In one giant leap, I was on top of him.

"OK, where is it?" I asked as I flipped him onto his back.

He didn't answer.

I gave him a shake. "Come on, I don't have all day."

"I don't know what you're talking about!" he shouted.

"Are all you criminals that stupid? I know you have it on you, it's just a matter of finding it. Here, I'll help." With one swipe of my claws, the hoodie, shirt and pants fell off his body.

"Oh look. Here it is," I mockingly exclaimed.

I took a step back and the guy looked up at me before fleeing, wearing only his tacky boxers and overpriced runners. I didn't bother going after him for several reasons. Those clothes weren't cheap, he was likely too scared I'd catch him if he tried stealing again, but most of all, I wanted to embarrass him.

I turned around with the device in my hand. Unable to resist the urge, I checked Robbie's current playlist, smiling while doing so.

"Thanks, Nightcat." A voice brought me back to the real world.

I looked up and there Robbie stood, a few paces away from me.

"Nightfall, actually," I corrected as I walked over to him.

Robbie was understandably confused.

"I ... I don't understand."

When I got closer to the overhead street light, he realized what I said was true.

"Are you like, her sister or something?" he asked.

"Nightcat and I are close, that much I can say." I'd leave him to his own conclusion. "Here's your MP3 player. You got quite a variety of songs on there."

Robbie was quite surprised. "You actually *know* these bands?"

"Well, I haven't met them, but I know who they are." I knew what he meant, but I couldn't resist.

We stood in awkward silence for the next minute.

"I, uh, should head out. Thanks for, you know ..." he said as he waved his MP3 player.

He took a few steps before turning back to me.

"Will I see you again? I mean, you'll be around, right?"

"Of course."

He gave a slight nod before he walked away.

Try as I might, I couldn't help but admire his butt. Hey, I can look, right?

A familiar voice addressed me.

"Sisters, hmm?"

I turned around to see my mom, in cat form. I wondered how long she had been standing there. Then the smile on her face told me she *knew*.

"So, how much of that did you see exactly?" I asked.

"Enough." Her smile then turned into an unclear expression.

"Look, I'm sorry, Mom. I didn't mean to lie to you about going home and finishing my homework. It's all done. It's just that I saw Robbie with Amanda, and I don't know what he sees in her cause it's like they ever hang around in school," I babbled.

Mom came forward and put her hands on my shoulders and gave them a small pat.

"You're not mad I followed him?"

"Somewhat," she replied. "But you were also in the right spot at the right time. And honestly, with how enhanced our senses are, it's pretty difficult *not* to accidentally eavesdrop."

"And you don't care that I was basically stalking him?"

"You were looking out for the wellbeing of a good friend, so no. Just next time, maybe dial it down a notch," she laughed. "And good job on that thug, by the way. I think your first solo adventure went pretty well."

"And you were watching the whole time, weren't you?"

"Do you honestly think you could sneak out of the house without me knowing, even in my human form? Mothers have enhanced senses too, you know."

Instinct

I did up as much of my paperwork as I could. I knew I'd have a few questions for Victor so I decided to combine them into one phone call. Quite frankly, the less I talked to him, the better.

I took a deep breath before dialling his extension. Most everyone in the company kept their distance from him, and I wasn't much different, except that my reasons had nothing to do with his micromanaging, egotistical personality and condescending attitude. Instead, it was that he was responsible for the creation of my alter ego, Nightcat. It had been many months since I was forced to go through that gruelling procedure, and I was still having nightmares about it.

Unlike my coworkers, however, I knew I could get away with a lot, and I pushed Victor as much and as far as I could. For the most part, I knew when to back off. His alter ego, a humanoid bat, was far stronger than me in my cat form. We had come to blows on more than one occasion, but of late we had found ourselves working together for a common cause.

Unexpectedly, I got his personal assistant on the phone. I was pretty much the only one that could phone him directly without her intercepting the call.

"Mr. Whitmoore's office, how may I help you?"

She was being unusually cheery and I assumed she picked up first before seeing my number on the caller ID.

"May I speak to Mr. Whitmoore, please?" It felt incredibly odd. I usually addressed him by his first name, not because we were friends but in hopes of annoying him, and it sort of stuck. But in the earshot of my coworkers, I had to at least pretend to be respectful.

"He isn't in the office. May I take a message?"

"Do you know when he'll be back?"

"He called in sick. He won't be in today and possibly tomorrow."

Another oddity. Victor's other half had a healing factor just like mine. Calling in sick was just an excuse to miss work.

"No, it's OK. I can send him an email."

"As you wish," she said, before hanging up.

Of course my mind ran amok and overanalyzed it all. I was sure it had something to do with his "extracurricular activities", though I couldn't figure out why he would call in sick. Why not just say he wasn't coming in? He wasn't in the habit of explaining his comings and goings to underlings.

I generally didn't care what he was doing, nor was I his babysitter, but the whole thing didn't seem right. I decided to try calling his cell. Thankfully I was one of the few people privy to the number.

It rang several times until his voicemail kicked in. Unsure what I would say, I decided nothing would be best. Besides, my number would show up on his phone so he'd know it was me.

As a last ditch effort, I tried calling his house and, just like his cell phone, it went to voicemail. Victor could handle himself, but my brain kept nagging at me to find out where he was. I wasn't going to get much more work done until I found him so I decided to leave work early. I was on salary, plus I tended to work a lot from home, so I didn't feel guilty leaving. The plus side of my job was that it required me to be out of the office on occasion so when something Nightcat-related came up, no one would question my absence.

Still, it would look odd if I suddenly wasn't in my office without anyone seeing me leave so I used the main entrance instead of my office window. I grabbed my personal effects to make it look legit. It was a good thing too, because I ran into my supervisor, Richard, on the way out.

"Hey Dana, on the way to a meeting?" he asked.

"Yeah, I'm not sure what time I'll be back and I might be out the rest of the day," I said before turning back to him in an afterthought. "I don't suppose you've seen Victor today, have you? I haven't been able to get hold of him."

"No, I haven't talked to him all day," he said, "although if you keep calling him by his first name he's likely to show up and overhear you." Even though Richard joked about it, he knew I was one of the few people at the office — no, make that the *only* person — who could get away with calling Victor by his first name.

I dumped my stuff in the back of the car and drove toward the lab, parking a few blocks away. After purposely locking my keys in the car I trotted down the nearest alleyway and morphed into Nightcat. It didn't take me too long to run the rest of the way to the lab. Its front door wasn't visible. Instead, it was hidden by a hologram to make it blend in with the rest of the building. I've been to the lab numerous times but it was still a bit of a guessing game as to where the door really was. Not that it mattered much because of the security cameras outside. After a few minutes of pacing back and forth the door still hadn't been made visible. I decided to knock on random spots on the wall. When that didn't work I started banging louder. It took a few minutes but my enhanced hearing heard shuffling on the other side. With a sci-fi swoosh, the door opened to reveal a very groggy Dr. Bertram in knee-high black socks and a white undershirt mostly obscured by a buttoned-up lab coat.

I stared at him for a moment before speaking.

"I guess this means I caught you at a bad time?" He gave me an ambiguous look. "Look, I'm really sorry to barge in on you like this but I need your help."

He waved me in and shut the door behind us.

"Not sure how much help I can be on two hours' sleep, but I'll try." Bertram escorted me to his office and he sat down in the chair and propped his head up with his hand.

"Have you heard from Victor at all today?" I asked.

Dr. Bertram gave me an odd look.

"Don't tell me you're actually concerned?" he said.

"I haven't heard from him all day and something doesn't feel right about it. Call it gut instinct."

"He hasn't been by the lab today and the last time I saw him he never mentioned anything."

"I don't suppose you have a tracking device embedded in him?" I half joked.

"No, but I can put a trace on a cell phone."

"Which won't be that accurate. Even *if* you tried phoning it and *if* I could hear it from here it'd still go to voicemail after 5 rings."

"I wasn't planning on phoning it." Bertram turned to face the keyboard and madly typed away. "It won't give an exact location but will point you in the right direction."

There wasn't much of a user interface displayed, but I understood a few of the commands that popped up on the screen. A few seconds later, he leaned forward and propped his glasses up higher on his nose. Obviously something intrigued him.

"What's up?" I asked.

Bertram didn't answer, but instead directed his attention back to the keyboard. I wasn't sure if he heard me or was merely lost in thought.

The display switched to a split screen, command code on the left side of the window and a satellite map on the right. I recognized some of the street names even though I wasn't overly familiar with the area.

Bertram muttered to himself incoherently.

"There," he pointed to the map. "That's where he was last at."

"How long ago?"

"About ... eight hours." He turned to me, worry evident on his tired face.

My concern outweighed my curiosity.

"I don't generally keep tabs on his whereabouts, but I'm assuming it isn't normal for Victor to just up and leave?" I asked.

"Most certainly not. He doesn't always inform me of the details, but it's uncharacteristic of him to be gone for this many hours."

"I guess I should go find him then, huh?" Not that I had any reason to ask. I was going to anyway.

"There is something you should know first." Bertram hesitated.

I tried to wait him out, but it didn't work. The geniuses were always socially inept.

"Which is?" I prodded.

"That's only a few blocks away from another lab."

"So what's the problem? You guys have more than one."

"This isn't *our* lab."

I sat there, silent as the dead. I knew there were others attempting to replicate the procedure that made me into Nightcat, though I had no idea how many competing labs were out there. With Raphael's help, I once broke into an "enemy" lab to save Bertram, who was being held prisoner. I wasn't sure how I'd manage it this time around.

"You're going to need some extra help, I imagine." It was like Bertram read my mind.

He walked me over to the other side of the room and placed his hand on a wall panel. I heard a bloop coming from the panel, obviously indicating he had a valid palm print. With a swoosh, part of the wall rose into the ceiling above and revealed a steel mannequin wearing what looked like part of a suit of armour.

I cocked my head to one side and stared at it. It was a dull grey and futuristic- looking although there were some key pieces missing. There weren't any gloves, and part of the upper arms, neckline, thighs and the bottom of the face were exposed. Even so, it looked like it had potential.

"No offense, but aren't you going to get injured in this thing? It doesn't look complete."

Bertram shook his head at me smirked.

"Oh, I didn't build it for me."

I was confused as to why he thought I'd need it.

"Umm, I have a healing factor, my true identity is a secret and I have super strength and reflexes. I'm not entirely sure how this is going to help."

Bertram reached over and grabbed a piece off the mannequin and handed it to me. As soon as it was close, the forearm piece opened up, easily allowing me to slide my arm into it. With a quick "click" it tightened up, fitting as if were specifically moulded to my arm. Which, I realized, it probably was.

"Well, that was unexpected," I said.

* * *

I surveyed the area from several buildings away, out of range of the lab's surveillance cameras. It didn't matter much because the suit of armour was equipped with some sort of cloaking technology. Any sensors wouldn't pick up on my heat signature and the cameras would return false visual information.

While the suit was surprisingly comfortable, the only real reason I agreed to wear it was for the cloaking feature, which Bertram explained was the only real completed tech it contained.

I surveyed the area, not that there was much to look at. The cameras were well hidden. I knew I couldn't go crashing in without a plan. There was no telling how many security personnel would be inside waiting for me. Bertram and I discussed it briefly before I left. The suit wasn't armed but he gave me some ad-hoc weaponry for this very purpose.

I had to be quick. I set several explosive devices on one side of the building, hustled to the other side, and laid the last charge. Knowing what was coming, I covered my ears, for what little good it would do.

As expected, security poured out the far side building like water from a ruptured dam. When the single charge went off nobody noticed in the commotion.

I slipped inside and immediately heard something that piqued my interest. It took a reasonable effort to smash through one of the inner walls. If the suit augmented my strength, it wasn't by much.

Before I even got in the room, I heard the panicked jingle of chains rattling. I looked over and saw Victor, who was obviously being "interrogated". Before even getting a word out, a security guard was closing in, gun pointed in my direction.

Thankfully the armour didn't impact my agility much. I dodged the shot, rendered his gun inoperable and I punched him in his helmeted face. As he fell over, my sixth sense started tingling. He was going for a sheathed knife strapped to his outer thigh. He didn't get very far. I grabbed it and slammed it down through his hand and into the floor beneath. The hilt of the knife would prevent him from simply running the blade through and regaining his freedom. I had no reason to kill him, nor did I want to, I only needed him disabled. Before he was able to let out a scream, I put him in a sleeper hold just long enough to make him pass out.

I next turned my attention to Victor and I saw the reason he didn't simply change into Raphael and escape. Not only was he chained, but it was like a double collar around his neck. The outer section had massive spikes and the inner section had holes for those spikes. If he had changed his added bulk would have burst the inner collar and driven the spikes into his neck.

His wrists and ankles were held in similar restraints. If there was a way for him to escape, it would have been extremely painful, and with a longer-than-usual recovery time. Our healing factors only worked in our alternate forms and it would have been extremely difficult to change while injured to that degree.

I easily broke the restraints and Victor would have fallen had I not caught him. They obviously had drugged him. It would have been the only way someone could have taken him prisoner.

He didn't respond so I lightly slapped his face until his eyes opened and he recognized me.

"How on earth ...?" he said.

"Your secretary said you called in sick, which from looking at you isn't far from the truth." He was banged up, though it didn't appear life-threatening. He just needed some time to muster up strength to change to his alter ego, at which point his healing factor would repair the damage.

He face was covered in cuts, all superficial save a nasty one over his right eyebrow. The blood had clotted, but not before leaving a reddish stripe down his face. They had torn his shirt and his chest was covered in deep cuts. They had been torturing him.

"Why did they do this to you?" I asked as I helped him to his feet.

"Perhaps we should discuss this at a more opportune time?" Victor stated.

He was right, of course. I hated that.

"Come one, let's get you back to Dr. Bertram."

Victor grabbed my shoulder.

"We cannot leave. There is unfinished business to attend to."

I wasn't sure if it was the exhaustion or his normal irritating personality that was making him speak in riddles.

"Kurt ..."

My anxiety rose. "What about him? He's at home."

"I would wager he is not," Victor said. "Have you performed a sweep of the other rooms in this facility?"

My eyes widened as I realized what he was getting at. Kurt was here too.

Something in my head snapped, and the rage spilled out of me. If anything had happened to Kurt, I would have reduced the building to rubble ... with everyone else inside.

Without a thought, I let go of Victor and he fell to his knees. It wasn't often I was this angry, but when I was, I'd either go into rage mode, or ultra-focused-not-speaking-to-anyone mode. This time it was the latter.

I turned away from Victor and casually walked through the large hole in the wall. As far as I was concerned, Victor could look after himself. It was no doubt his fault Kurt was here.

I speed-walked the hallways and the few guards that tried to stop me had their knees and elbows inverted. It required no effort on my part, and while time was of the essence, I knew having a whole building of security personnel coming after me would jeopardize my chances of finding Kurt and getting us out alive.

It was then I actually remembered the armour. My one-way thinking forgot about it at first so I pushed the button on my helmet, near the temple to bring up the heads-up display. I wasn't sure of the suit's capabilities so I started spewing out commands on the off chance one would work.

"Show me the floor plan of this building."

"Insufficient data."

Dammit.

"Can you tell me where the rest of the guards are?"

"Insufficient data."

Double dammit.

"Can you tell me how many guards are in the building?"

"Insufficient data."

Triple dammit.

"Do you think you could possibly show me show me the heat signatures of the people in this building?" I was getting frustrated and my voice sounded more like a growl when I spoke.

The computer didn't answer verbally, but through the visor I saw ghost-like reddish images. At least the hardware was capable of this.

I scanned the area and the red blobs were starting to converge. There was one blob, more orange than red and all alone. It had to be Kurt.

Without knowing the building layout, I decided the best way was to punch through walls. My armour, anger and augmented strength made it quite easy, regardless how reinforced the walls were.

As I barrelled through the last wall, I saw Kurt. For a minute I thought he was dead, then I realized he couldn't have been because his heat signature would have been much lower, or non-existent.

"Kurt?"

He strained his neck to look up then immediately recoiled in fear as I ran over to him.

"It's OK, Kurt, it's me." I proceeded to haul off the helmet and toss it aside. "I'm here."

We hugged for a second before I broke his restraints and helped him get his footing. He wasn't in the greatest shape, but he was better than Victor had been. Presumably they needed information from Victor and Kurt was their leverage.

After one step, Kurt's knees buckled out from under him. If it hadn't been for my enhanced strength and speed, I wouldn't have been able to catch him in time.

I gently sat him down and mentally kept alert for any danger coming out way.

"I'm slowing you down," Kurt said quietly.

"You're the reason I'm here," I half lied. Up until ten minutes ago I had been here for Victor.

I saw Kurt started to fade into unconsciousness. I gave his cheek a light slap, trying to bring him out of it. When that didn't work, I started hollering his name, not caring if I drew any attention to us.

An idea then struck. It was something I had tried only once before, and it wasn't with Kurt.

I quickly reverted to my human form, the armour falling off as soon as I started the process. I wasn't sure what would become of it when I changed, but I didn't care.

"Kurt, I want you to focus. You need to change to Prodigy to heal. I'll help."

A while back it happened by accident. I had morphing issues and I unknowingly caused Paige, another one of Victor's test subjects, to revert to her human self.

Kurt's eyes fluttered and he opened his mouth to say something, but I cut him off.

"I know you don't like it, but there's no other way."

He smiled a half smile. "I *was* going to say thanks."

I quickly grabbed him by the hand, knowing both our lives were in danger while in human form. I closed my eyes and tightened my grip. I started the change, mentally trying to "pass over" to Kurt. This was the first time I had consciously tried to help someone else change.

I felt fur sprouting from the back of Kurt's hand and the ripple of the transformation ran up his arm. My morph was going slower. No doubt the nanites were concentrating on Kurt's transfiguration first, which was fine by me.

Before I had completed the morph for myself, I heard a large thud behind me and Prodigy recoiled, causing my own change to stop, then reverse completely.

There stood Victor, or rather, Raphael, in the custom "door" I made earlier. One gun-carrying security guard was slumped off to the side, out cold. Or worse.

Wide-eyed, I stared at Raphael. He didn't look completely healed, but he was in a lot better shape than in his human form.

"Thanks, but we'll take it from here," I said as I helped Prodigy to his feet.

"Do not let the size of your ego lead you to decline assistance," Raphael said, his voice weary.

"Look, Kurt wouldn't be in this mess it weren't for you!" The anger in me started to rise.

"You are correct. However, he might have been dead had I not intervened." Raphael turned and looked behind him, obviously hearing something I couldn't.

"We must flee while we are still able," he said.

* * *

Back at Raphael's lab, Bertram ran a slew of medical scans on Prodigy. Raphael and I were in the adjacent room watching through the two-way mirror.

"Do not worry, his healing abilities are at the very least equal to ours." Raphael uncharacteristically placed his hand on my shoulder, in an effort to put my mind at ease.

I looked up at him. "I know, I just worry. It's my job to keep him safe, and I couldn't even do that."

"Our dear Kurt does have two parents, or have you forgotten?" Raphael half smiled.

Victor had to maintain a distance from Kurt, in order to keep our secret identities safe, but on rare occasions, he was there for Kurt when he needed it most. This was one of those times.

"Thank you for looking out for him," I said sincerely. "But you still haven't told me what happened."

"It does not matter, as the situation shall be resolved." Raphael then turned his attention back to Kurt.

"If I don't know what happened, how am I supposed to protect him? How many of these other labs are there and why do they need us so badly?"

"The experiments conducted at our laboratory were, even now, ground breaking. And not easily duplicated, the good doctor made sure of that. There have been several others that have tried to duplicate his procedure, but none have been successful. And rightfully so. Dr. Bertram is quite protective of his findings and is the pioneer in his field. No other comes close to matching his intellect."

Raphael hadn't told me anything useful so I waited him out.

"There are those with the misconception that this technology should be available for all. And in order to obtain the information they desire, they will not hesitate to use drastic measures."

"And by that you mean using Kurt to get to you."

"I assure you, Ms. Harker, it shan't happen a second time. I shall personally see to it."

"Not without me you aren't."

"It would be best if you did not participate, Ms. Harker, as I do not believe you would approve of my methods," he said, and I couldn't disagree with him on that point.

I was still in shock that Raphael would put his life on the line to save Kurt's. I knew I had protective motherly instincts when it came to Kurt, I always had, but it really said something about Raphael's character that he had similar parental instincts.

No Costumes Required

"I'm home!" I exclaimed as I dumped my backpack on the floor with a loud *thud*. Neither of my parents answered, which was odd because both vehicles were in the driveway. They should have been home.

Actually I lie. Mom could very well be out superhero-ing it up with Dad, a sergeant in the Grace City Police Department, by her side. Once upon a time the cars would have been a good indicator they were home, but not now. It didn't bother me at all, honestly. I was rather excited when I found out not only was my mother Grace City's very own Nightcat, but that I had also inherited her feline form.

I headed to the kitchen to grab an after-school snack, and found my parents sitting in the dining room with a large printed map spread out across the table.

"What'cha doing?" I asked.

"The world's biggest search engine company asked us to hand-draw their updated maps," Mom looked at me with a half smile.

"Uh huh." Aside from the ridiculousness of the claim, Mom couldn't draw a stick man with a ruler. I pulled out a chair and sat down, getting a better look at the map, which happened to be of Grace City.

"What's with all the coloured dots all over the place?" I asked.

"These are the locations of all the DUI and noise complaints over the past several years," Mom said.

"OK, but what's it *for*?"

"It's so we can find trends between party locations in the city and drunk drivers that have been arrested in the past," Dad said.

It was obviously to help them when they were out on patrol.

"But why would a superhero do that? No offence, Mom, but can't Dad do that? Besides, it's not Christmas or New Year's Eve, and Halloween is more than a week away."

"The adult Halloween parties tend to happen the weekend before. Honestly, unless Halloween falls on a weekend, the weekend before it is usually busier."

"So when are we going out?" I asked.

Mom looked over at Dad so I gave him a big hug to butter him up. He looked down at the table for a moment and let out a sigh. As he slowly looked up I could see the grin on his face.

"You'd best ask your mom that question," he replied.

Bubbling over with excitement, I practically knocked her over with a mid-collision hug.

"Can-I-go? Can-I-go? Can-I-go?"

"Maybe." She seemed far less happy about the idea than Dad.

I slumped down in one of the chairs and unconsciously started to pout. "Maybe" generally meant "No".

"I don't see the big deal," I said. "It's not like we'd be battling super-villains. It could be a good training exercise for me."

"Sarah," Mom started. "It's not as simple as that ..."

"Sure it is, you're just *making* it hard."

Dad put his hand on my shoulder, which got my attention. The look on his face told me not to pursue the matter.

"I'm sorry, Mom. I just don't understand why you're so hesitant, that's all." I said sincerely.

Mom took her time answering me. It was like she was reliving a past trauma and it was starting to manifest as tears.

"It's not that I think you couldn't handle it physically. I just know that car accidents can lead to a lot of emotional scarring and I don't want you to have to go through that."

Now I was really curious what happened. It sounded like she was speaking from experience.

* * *

The next day during a spare period at school, I Googled "Nightcat DUI" but didn't come back with many hits. They were all just about how many drunk drivers Nightcat had caught along with a ton of stats showing the decline in deaths and injuries since Mom became Nightcat.

That got me thinking. If *Nightcat* didn't have the traumatic experience, then perhaps it was my *mother*. Was she in a car accident? Was she physically hurt? Was she with someone who got hurt? Or was she the drunk driver and was hiding it from me out of guilt? I knew she wasn't telling me everything and while I found it difficult to think she'd be that careless, she also wasn't much of a drinker either. Or one to go to parties. Still, I had to find out.

I didn't have much time left in my spare so I gathered up my stuff and headed to my next class. History was pretty boring at the best of times, so I sat there thinking about various scenarios and what I should try Googling. It occurred to me that I was focusing on my mother when it was more likely someone both my parents knew. I had to start with the most plausible scenario first and at lunch hour I launched another search; this time for "Dana Harker DUI", my working theory being that she was in the car that was hit. I scrolled through a half dozen pages of results before taking a break. My eyes were starting to see double and I knew I'd have to sift through many more pages before getting my answer. The incident would have happened years ago, possibly even before I was born, so it wasn't going to be on the first few pages of hits.

An hour and about 50 pages later I still hadn't found anything, so I decided something else: "Harker car". A few articles down was something that looked promising enough to be worth a click. My excitement quickly fell when a stupid pop-up showed on my screen saying I'd have to buy a subscription to view the archives. I resisted the urge to fling my laptop across the room and sat there mentally calming myself.

After a minute or so an idea came to me: I'd buy a prepaid credit card and use that to pay for the stupid subscription. I opened up another tab in my browser so I wouldn't lose my spot. Virtual card in virtual hand, I signed up and entered in the numbers. After a tense five seconds of waiting for approval, it went through. Once again my excitement was overflowing.

I skimmed the article but nothing jumped out at me until the very end. It was an update to the article mentioning the deceased's name: Clarice Harker. The last name couldn't have been a coincidence. I then read the full article intently.

The more I read, the more horrified I got. An unnamed drunk driver was coming back from a house party and slammed into a vehicle stopped at a stop sign. The driver had no injuries, but the occupants of the other car weren't so lucky. Alex Harker suffered minor injuries, but his wife Clarice died on scene.

It was then I knew why this made Mom so emotional. This was her brother and his wife ... my aunt.

The article was dated almost six years before I was born, so I had never even met my aunt, not even as a baby. That really hurt. And I had no idea why she was never mentioned in any family conversations before. Why would Mom and Dad have kept this from me? Obviously Uncle Alex had someone in his life at some point in time because he had Rachel, who used to babysit me when she was home from university.

With lunch hour almost over, I phoned my brother, who unsurprisingly picked up on the first ring.

"Kurt!" It came out louder than I thought and I'm sure he had to pull his phone away from his ear when he answered.

"Sarah? Sarah? I can't hear you!" he joked.

"Sorry to make this short, but can you meet me after school?"

"Of course. Is something wrong?" he asked, his voice full of concern.

"No, not really, I'm fine I just ..." The warning bell sounded. Crap.

"I can pick you up from school if you like and we can talk then," he said.

"Sure ... and can you not tell Mom I called?"

"Sarah, what are you hiding?" he asked.

"Nothing, I promise it's nothing bad, I just have some stuff to ask, that's all."

"OK, I'll pick you up, but let Mom know so she doesn't freak when you're not at home right away."

The second bell rang, making me officially late. Double crap.

"Gotta go, and I'll call her. I promise!"

* * *

Before I ran to the main doors after school, I texted Mom to let her know I'd be late. She wasn't terribly overprotective, especially with me having superpowers, but she and Dad liked to know where I was. After hitting "Send" I checked my unread messages. There was a text from Kurt letting me know where he was. My school wasn't terribly huge, but once the last bell rang for the day it was like a madhouse, and it would have taken me a while to find him in the parking lot.

As soon as I spotted him standing outside of his car, he waved. I ran over and gave him a big hug. We didn't grow up together and weren't full-blooded siblings, but it didn't matter. I was and always will be his baby sister much in the same way as he has always been my more-than-slightly-overprotective big brother.

"So kiddo, what's up?"

My smile turned to an instant frown. I really wasn't sure how to explain it all to him.

Kurt's expression turned to shock. "Oh my God, you're pregnant."

"*What*? Gah! No! How could you even think that?"

Kurt breathed a sigh of relief.

"Can we sit in the car?" I asked, once the red left my face.

"Sure," he said as he opened the passenger side door. I sat there fidgeting while he came around and settled in the driver's seat.

"I need to ask you something about our family. Mom didn't give me much info about it and honestly I didn't really ask 'cause it seemed pretty upsetting to her."

Kurt sat there intently. "I'll do what I can."

"Did you know Aunt Clarice?"

Kurt nodded slightly, not in agreement, but as an acknowledgement of what I had to ask.

"You're wanting to know more about her, aren't you?"

"Yeah."

"Sadly, I never met her, she died even before I was born. I only know her from what I've been told."

"How did she die?" I asked quietly. I needed to confirm the article's authenticity. Plus, above all, I wanted to hear it from a family member.

Kurt took a minute before answering. "Drunk driver, but since you're asking about her, you probably know that part because it's public record."

"I found that out from Google, but I was wondering if that was it? Like, I know it sucks but why does Mom act like she feels guilty? She wasn't even Nightcat then so how could it have been her fault?"

"It wasn't." Kurt sat there like he was mustering up the courage to continue on. "Keep in mind this is only what I've been told. Our aunt and uncle weren't big drinkers and would usually take turns being the designated driver. That New Year's it was Uncle Alex's turn to be DD but Aunt Clarice volunteered. They got hit by an underaged drunk driver on the way home and she died at the scene. Uncle Alex never fully recovered psychologically. He never dated again, never remarried, nothing. And the worst thing of all was that because the driver was underage, he basically got away with it."

I might have only been a partial red-head, but my inner ginger rage burned inside of me. How on any planet would that have been considered justice?

"I'm sorry," Kurt said as he gave me a hug.

"It's not your fault, I'm just glad you told me," I said. "Why am I just finding this out now? Like, why this big secret?"

"I don't think it was meant to be the big secret it became. It's just not something that's ever brought up in conversation because it's too painful. Even after all this time."

We sat there in silence for a few minutes before Kurt spoke again.

"I know it's not much, but maybe some ice cream will help?"

I smiled at him. "Only if you're buying."

* * *

After some long overdue quality sibling time with Kurt, I asked to be dropped off at the nearest mall. As soon as I discovered the details about Aunt Clarice, I had a kernel of an idea form in my head.

I needed to know more about that idiot kid that killed her. I mean, he could have been my age for all I knew. And while I didn't drive, I knew, even before all of this, the devastation one stupid mistake like that could mean. I couldn't wrap my brain around why someone would be so dumb and take the risk.

Because he was underage, the media wouldn't have released his name. And it's not like I could hack into the police files or ask my father for the information. *I* couldn't get the info. But *Nightcat* could — or at least someone who looked like her.

The biggest difference between us, on first glance anyway, was the hair colour. In my human form I had a mix of my parents' hair colours so I came out as a strawberry blonde. Nightfall's was a charcoal grey in colour, which I found odd. Mom's hair was red, albeit a little less red over the years, while Nightcat's hair was a rust colour. Not wanting a permanent colour or the mess and fuss of a dye job, I went to one of the stores in the mall and bought a reasonably-priced rust-coloured Halloween wig.

The first part of my unfinished master plan had been completed. I just needed to figure out the rest of it.

* * *

I smuggled the wig into the house in my backpack and after a quick "Hello" and "I have to do my homework" to my parents, I scurried to my room.

Behind the safety of my closed bedroom door, I changed into Nightfall. The microscopic computers that ran in my bloodstream, as well as my mother's, were what gave us the ability to change our physical structures. Fur the colour of milk chocolate covered my body, pointed elven-like ears replaced the roundness of human ears, a semi-prehensile tail sprouted from my backbone, my lower legs became cat-like, a black costume ... which got me thinking. My costume was slightly different from Nightcat's. Both costumes were like strapless low-backed one-piece bathing suits with swirls in the cup area, but mine had three points where Mom's only had two. And where Mom's costume had a slit all the way down to her navel, mine had a bit of material in the middle holding the two front pieces together.

As much as I hated the idea, I needed to be as accurate as possible, and that meant modifying my costume. I'd deal with the repercussions later. I thumbed through my desk drawer looking for some scissors. As far as I could tell the costume's fabric wasn't woven so it shouldn't fray. I breathed a little sigh before cutting into my costume to make it more Nightcat-like. A half hour later after much picky work, and viewing reference photos for accuracy, I finished the alterations.

I tied my long hair in a loose ponytail, flipped it upside my head and placed the newly christened wig on my head. After tucking a few loose strands of hair in, I grabbed a hand mirror to have a peek. My new look was far better than any store-bought Nightcat Halloween costume, but it wasn't perfect. That being said, I didn't have to look *exactly* like my mother, just a passable facsimile.

Satisfied with the likeness, I changed back to my human form, did my homework and then spent the evening with my folks and acting as normally as I could.

* * *

It wasn't easy, but I got up at around 4:30 in the morning. I didn't dare set my alarm to ring, so I set it to vibrate only and taped it to my hand so I'd feel it go off. I couldn't have my parents know what I was up to. I quickly and quietly changed to my feline form.

With my enhanced hearing, I gave a quick listen to the room next door and could hear two resting heartbeats accompanied by deep breathing. I knew my parents were sleeping and hadn't gotten up in the middle of the night for anything police - or superhero - related.

Just like I had practiced, I tucked my hair under the wig and before heading out, had another quick peek at my reflection to make sure everything was in place. Much to my surprise, my costume was back to its regular style. The modifications I had made earlier didn't take!

Trying not to let my temper get the best of me, I took a few deep breaths. I didn't have time to make the costume perfect again. I needed to get to the police station before my father, and the earlier I got there, the better. For all I knew he (and possibly my mother as Nightcat) would be called in.

I had another idea: go to Mom's hideout and grab one of her spare costumes. Luckily it was on the way to the police station so I wouldn't lose much time. I quietly opened my bedroom window and slipped out into the cool autumn night.

* * *

Not long after discovering my abilities, Mom showed me her hideout. I didn't know the whole story about how she acquired it, but I knew it was a refuge of sorts for her. It looked like it was a gym back in the day. It still had older exercise equipment in it. Not that Nightcat would have needed it, but Mom told me that her feline abilities were proportional to her human abilities. The stronger she was in human form, the stronger Nightcat was. Even though Mom was pushing 50, she was in great shape. She mentioned that she and Dad would often train together so neither one lost their edge. Dad may have been more of a desk-jockey than years ago, but he knew the value of exercise and didn't want to be "that cop".

The hideout was like a second home for Mom. The main area had basic furnishings, couch, chair and even a small kitchen. There was a chest of drawers near the couch that Mom kept a change of clothes in, as well as a spare costume or two.

I climbed out of my costume and slipped into hers, only to realize it was a tad too big. Mom and I had the same build, but I was also still a teen and didn't, well, fill it out completely.

With one hand holding the costume up, I rummaged through the drawer hoping to find something that would help, a box of Kleenex or something.

"I'm such an idiot," I muttered to myself. "Why was *this* the best plan I had?"

I continued to look, my mind thinking of a million things at once — the costume, how I was going to pull this off — when I heard something unfamiliar to me. I looked down and noticed a difference in the fit. I went over to the full length mirror and slowly took my hand away. The costume didn't fall. It had reshaped itself to my body.

The nanites were responsible for morphing clothing to the costume, so they must have had something to do with it. When I first changed to Nightfall, Mom went under the assumption that our powers were the same until we discovered otherwise. I mentally filed this new information away for later.

I had one last look in the mirror before leaving and let out a grunt of frustration. I was tired and cranky and just noticed another thing that was amiss.

Not ever forgetting time was of the essence, I bounded to the kitchen area and scoured through the cabinets, looking for a Sharpie. Mom had *four* black stripes on her upper thigh, but I only had three. The Sharpie made quick work of adding another.

Satisfied, I took off to the police station as quickly as I could.

* * *

Thankfully, I didn't see Dad's car in the parking lot so it was highly unlikely that he had been called in. Breathing a sigh of relief, I scaled the wall to the third floor window and knocked gently on it. It was my mother's signature move, but it was also the only way I knew how to get into the station.

One of the communications officers was on the phone, but the other one came over to the window and opened it up. I mustered all my courage and pretended to be my mother. (How many teenagers would willingly do that?)

I climbed in and almost started introducing myself as Nightcat.

Like they don't already know who you are, dummy.

"Hey, Nightcat. What can I help you with?"

I didn't know this dude so I looked down at his name badge.

Look at me go! I'll be a detective someday! I mused

"Thanks, Briggs. I'm trying to get some information on a really old case."

"How old is old?" he asked as he sat back down at his desk.

"Like 21 years ago, give or take," I answered in my best Nightcat voice.

"Do you have a name or incident so I can narrow it down?"

"Yeah." I tried not to let my suppressed emotions spill out. Had to remain professional. "A husband and wife were in a car accident with an underaged driver. The wife didn't make it."

"Names?" Briggs asked.

"I don't have them, unfortunately. But it did happen around New Year's if that helps." I had the names, but if he could find the information without me telling him it would bring more credibility to my request.

"No problem, I can do a search without it." He pushed his glasses higher up on his nose and hunched closer to the screen, pressing the down arrow every couple of seconds.

"There's a few here that I can find.

"That's perfect!" I said with a bit too much enthusiasm. "I'm helping David with some old cases." Man, it was weird referring to my dad by his first name. I only did so because my mother never called him by rank.

"I can beam the info to you."

"That'd be great." I hauled out my nanoMyte and a second later the information was transferred.

I unfolded the screen to make it bigger and took a quick glance. It was just what I needed. I safely tucked it away to review it fully later on.

"Thanks for the help!" I said as I plunged out the window. I barely made out a "You're welcome" from him 'cause I was long gone.

I made myself comfortable on the roof of a nearby building and opened up my nanoMyte device. There were a lot of virtual pages in the file so I took a quick browse before digging in. The kid's name was Matthew "Matt" Hill. He was 15 at the time of the accident and was driving his parents' "borrowed-without-permission" Mercedes. He was intoxicated, approximately three times over the legal limit, doing 100km/h in a 50 zone and hit my aunt and uncle's stopped vehicle. The driver's side was completely obliterated, while the passenger's side was only marginally damaged. The driver, Clarice Harker, died on impact, and her husband Alex Harker was taken to the hospital with minor injuries. The most serious of Uncle Alex's injuries, other than a broken heart over losing his wife, were a broken arm and a concussion. I was only able to look at a few of the accident photos before putting the file away. The last thing I wanted was to stumble across the coroner's photographic findings.

I sat there sobbing gently over the loss over something I never knew I had up until a day ago, and ended up crying myself to sleep.

* * *

I woke to my mother's voice calling my name in a stage whisper. I remembered falling asleep on a roof so I had no idea why she was trying to be subtle.

I opened my eyes to find her standing in front of me, looking very upset. It was rare I saw my mother angry, but when she was fired up it was kinda scary, even more so when she was in her feline form.

I had no idea what to say to her, so I just sat there.

"I know what you did, Sarah, I just don't know why." Mom crossed her arms and simply glared at me.

I looked downward, avoiding eye contact.

"Your father went into work this morning and found out that *I* was there requesting information on an old Harker family tragedy. I also got a call from the school saying you hadn't shown up yet. That was at nine o'clock."

My eyes widened. What time was it, anyway?

"Your father is waiting for you at the police station. He'll take you home and we can discuss this as a family."

"I ... I'm really sorry, Mom. You weren't supposed to find out."

Idiot! That's was totally the wrong thing to say!

"It still would have been wrong even if I *didn't* find out," she said.

Suddenly, I heard a high pitched wail and instinctively put my hands over my ears.

"What's that?" I hollered.

Mom turned her head in the general direction of the noise. It didn't seem to bother her much.

"Bank alarm. It's broadcasting at a frequency only we can hear so if I'm nearby I can help." Mom looked back at me. "This doesn't change anything. Your father is waiting and we'll discuss this at home when I get back."

She rushed off, leaving me standing there.

My brain was in overdrive. I still wanted to help Mom out, regardless how much more trouble I'd get into. She always said that she was given her powers for a reason and didn't like the idea of squandering them. I thought the same of mine.

* * *

When I got to the bank it looked like Mom had rounded up the hostages and was defending them. The robbers had a gun pointed in her direction. Mom was there, arms wide, as if to shield the people behind her.

I had to act fast, so I took the main guy out. I toppled him over but lost focus when I heard Mom yell my name. I looked over to her and suddenly my sixth sense went off like a beacon. Looking out of the corner of my eye, I saw a gun pointed at my head. As fast as I was, I wasn't sure if I could dodge it without getting my brains splattered everywhere.

The robber sneered. "So you know her?" he said to Mom.

Mom moved forward slightly, hands in front of her, almost as if she was surrendering.

"Look, you don't want to do this," she said quietly as she walked closer. He responded by putting the barrel closer to my head. I started tearing up, unsure if Mom had a plan. This wasn't supposed to happen. I was supposed to help her, not the other way around. I came in and just made it worse. Like I always do.

"If you let her go, I won't follow you," Mom offered.

The robber was skeptical. "How do I know you're not lying?"

"You don't. You just have to trust me."

The robber took a minute, and slowly pointed his gun at my mother instead.

"Nightfall, go!" she hollered at me.

I took a minute, but as soon as Mom had that look on her face, I knew I better get away.

* * *

I sat there on the Jade River Bridge, feet dangling over, my tears adding to the depth of the water below. It didn't matter where I was, it was only a matter of time before my mother found me. Assuming she was even still alive.

I was noisily sobbing away and only noticed Mom when she placed her hand on my shoulder. Surprisingly, she sat down next to me.

"The view is quite pretty this time of year," she said, staring off into the distance.

I said nothing but continued to cry uncontrollably for another ten minutes.

"You're not dead!" I stammered when I finally caught my breath.

"Of course I'm not," she scoffed. "That was hardly the most dangerous situation I was ever in."

"I'm sorry I made it worse."

"You didn't make it worse. I was more concerned with your safety than anything else."

We sat there in silence for a minute or two.

"You know we have to talk, right, Sarah?" Mom said gently.

Through tear-blurred eyes I looked at her and nodded, thankful I couldn't see the details of her expression. I was psyching myself up for the worst.

"You're not going to let me be Nightfall again, are you?"

Mom sighed, and I feared her next words. "I'd be lying if I didn't say it hadn't occurred to me, but I'm more curious why you did what you did."

It was one of the things I loved about my mom. Even when I was being disciplined, she was still compassionate and never rushed doling out a punishment. I knew I still had a lot to answer for, but that didn't stop Mom from putting her arm around me and giving me a warm hug. Even if she wasn't in her superhero form, her hugs always made me felt safe.

"What were you going to do with the information about Clarice's death?"

I started bawling again. "I don't know. I just knew I needed to find out."

"You could have asked."

"But that night with you and Dad ... you didn't go into detail."

"No, only because it took me by surprise and I honestly wasn't sure how to approach it right then. Your father and I talked that night trying to figure out how to tell you."

I wiped away a tear with the palm of my hand.

"Why was it such a family secret?"

"It wasn't supposed to be, it just sort of happened. Alex still mourns her death to this day, so to spare him the pain of having to relive the event, it's not something we talk about," Mom said quietly.

"Kurt said Uncle Alex took it pretty hard."

Mom stared at me with a raised eyebrow.

"I wasn't going to chance asking you again, so I asked Kurt. He told me what he knew."

"I see." I'm not sure if Mom was disappointed I talked to Kurt or the fact I talked to him when it should have been her talking to me. "And what did he tell you?"

I relayed to her what Kurt told me earlier.

"That's more or less it," Mom replied. "It happened several months before I was Nightcat, but when your dad and I got together and he talked about parties, specifically the then-upcoming Halloween parties, I volunteered to help. It was my hope that I could at least make a positive impact. Between that and occasionally going to the high schools and talking about the effects of impaired driving, I felt that Clarice's death wasn't in vain."

"But what about the driver? The report said his time was minimal. That's hardly justice."

"I agree that the young offenders act needs work, but it's not up to us to make that decision by ourselves, being in the role that we're now in." I knew she was talking about us being superheroes. "We can't seek out revenge. We have to be above that and set a good example for the citizens of Grace City. Nothing good ever comes out of revenge."

Mom and I sat there for a bit and I could smell the salt in her tears.

"We can't change the past, but we can change the future."

"And mine no doubt includes a decade of grounding," I frowned.

"I think that would be a bit much."

I looked up at my Mom to see if she was serious.

"The fact of the matter is that what you did was wrong, even if you didn't mean any harm by it. We can talk about it more later on, but for now I think it best if we go home and have a nice hot meal."

"Is me having to eat your cooking part of my punishment?" I asked.

Nightfall
by Jim Robb

She did not wake until the sun rose above the tops of the pines and cast its bright light through the window. Silently she slipped out of bed and padded towards the bathroom, stopping on the way to pick up the garment she had abandoned on the floor the evening before. It resembled a black one-piece bathing suit, strapless, cut low in the back, with an inch-wide slit down the front ending in a diamond-shaped opening at the navel. It would have been a daring outfit indeed, were it not for the fur that covered her body.

Closing the bathroom door behind her, she paused to look at herself in the mirrored shower door. Her face was covered in the same soft, dark brown fur as her body. Her ears extended upward to points that peeked through reddish brown hair, which in front formed bangs that ended just above her eyes, and in back extended past her shoulder blades. The fur was accented with black markings, three stripes on each arm and calf and four on each thigh, which came to points as they neared the front of each long limb. Her tail was visible as it curved gracefully upward above her right shoulder. In this form she was known as Nightcat.

In human form she was Dana Harker, but she hadn't been in human form for more than six years. She had stopped being Dana Harker shortly after she had started experiencing chest pains which reminded her of the procedure that had given her the ability to change forms.

Although Trinity Summers was a pediatrician, she knew more about her best friend's altered physiology than anyone alive. "It was a heart attack," she told Dana, "and it wasn't your first. But the next one will almost certainly be your last."

It was Trinity, too, who had suggested the means by which Dana had extended her life. Dana's bloodstream carried nanites, microscopic computerized robots that gave her the ability to change forms, and which kept her alive during the radical changes to her physiology brought about by the metamorphosis.

As a side benefit, the nanites provided her body with greatly enhanced healing powers while she was Nightcat. So long as Dana remained in her feline form, her healing factor would keep her heart from failing.

It hadn't been hard for Dana's husband, David Rayner, to convince her she should act on Trinity's suggestion and become Nightcat full-time. Dana and David had been together for many years and were still as deeply in love as they had been almost from the day they met. The thought of leaving him alone was reason enough for Dana to give up her human form permanently. But more than that, Dana, who was then only in her mid-fifties and looked twenty years younger, simply wasn't ready for her time on earth to end just yet. "After all," she had joked to Trinity, "being Nightcat from now on isn't a fate worse than death."

This was true enough, but she hadn't been especially comfortable about it either. She had not been comfortable with her feline form in the beginning, when she had been abducted and forced to endure the horrific experiment that had turned her into a were-cat. She hadn't been comfortable being Nightcat, the reluctant superhero, when people she had saved had frequently been more afraid of her than the truly monstrous sociopaths she had saved them from. In fact, the only time she had been truly comfortable as Nightcat was in David's arms, but she had always felt truly comfortable there, whatever her form.

David had surprised her last night. "A cat should never tease an old dog," he said afterwards. "It might have one bite left." So she took a shower, and dried off by shaking herself before slipping into her costume. She returned to the bedroom to find David still in bed, eyes tightly closed and face averted from the sunlight.

"Would you like me to fix us breakfast?" she asked, knowing full well what his reaction would be.

"No, no," he said in feigned distress, "anything but that. You go for your romp, and it'll be on the table when you get back."

She kissed him on the special place on his neck just below and behind his ear, the spot she alone knew about, and quickly danced out of his reach and through the bedroom door.

She glided quietly to the living room and stopped to admire the view out the large front windows. When she had accepted that she would have to be Nightcat for the rest of her life, it had been obvious to both of them they couldn't continue to live in Grace City. They continued to rent out Dana's condominium apartment, and their daughter had bought David's house, which she had always loved, for its fair value. The proceeds of these two transactions, augmented by a surprisingly small fraction of their considerable savings, had paid for a house on a large acreage in the mountains several miles from a small town. Dana continued to receive quarterly dividends on the shares she held in the very successful computer consulting company of which she was a co-founder. David, who was nine years Dana's senior, had enough years of service with the police department that he was able to retire with a full pension. From these sources of income their simple but comfortable lifestyle was well within their means. They both wanted to leave their savings for their children, both of whom possessed Dana's shapeshifting abilities.

Dana emerged from her trip down memory lane as she entered the kitchen. Her gaze settled on the knife block on the counter, and the paring knife with which she had accidentally cut herself a few weeks ago. Her healing factor should have caused the wound to close immediately. Instead, it had bled for several minutes. This time she didn't need Trinity to tell her what the problem was. Her heart had deteriorated to the point where the nanites had to concentrate on keeping it running, and no longer had the capacity to deal with less important matters. She knew it would not be long now before they would be unable to cope with the task of keeping her alive.

Still, she had the present, which was really all anyone had. And right now, she was wasting it. She let herself out the door at the back of the kitchen, leaped over the deck rail, rapidly crossed the large back lawn, and bounded along the path leading up the mountain.

For short distances Nightcat could maintain highway speed, but instead she loped along at an easy pace for her, although it would have outstripped any human sprinter's best effort. The local wildlife knew from long experience she wasn't a danger to them, and they ignored her presence as she moved swiftly through the forest. Nor did she worry about what she might meet in the forest, for her genetically-enhanced strength, cat-quick reactions, speed, uncanny agility, razor-sharp claws, and the weaponry housed in her dark metal wrist cuffs made her far more than a match for any predator she might encounter, here or anywhere else.

The path led through the heavily-wooded hillside toward a high mountain stream near the back of the property. The stream was at the bottom of a vertical rock face a hundred feet high, a difficult challenge even for an experienced climber. Nightcat didn't even break stride. She skittered down the cliff head first, driving her claws into the hard stone to support her. She splashed along the stream for several hundred feet, then scampered effortlessly back up the sheer rock.

Now she moved through the trees, trying not to touch the ground, sometimes jumping from tree to tree, sometimes using the grapples housed in her wrist cuffs to swing between the trees. When she ran out of trees she dropped to the lawn and ran the last hundred yards at full speed, ending by jumping back over the railing onto the wide back deck of the house.

She paused there, not to catch her breath, but to marvel at the wonders of the forest she had just run through. Beautiful by any standards, it was even more so when experienced through the enhanced senses that were hers, for her sight, hearing and sense of smell were far beyond human norms. She had not used her powers for simple enjoyment until she had started going on these morning runs, and she now found the experience exhilarating. She had never felt more alive, more happy, more content with her lot than she did at that moment. Truly, life was good.

* * *

The bedroom window was still open, and she used it to re-enter the house. She would have to take another shower before breakfast, because David disliked the feel and smell of sweaty fur. Surprisingly, David was still in bed. "Come on, sleepyhead, I'm back. Where's breakfast?" she said over her shoulder as she padded to the bathroom.

David didn't respond. Nightcat turned and walked slowly back toward the bed, reaching out with her enhanced sight and hearing. She detected no breathing, no heartbeat, no movement, no sign of life. Kneeling beside the bed, she slowly reached out and touched his face. Then she put her face against his shoulder and wept silently.

After a time she stood and backed away from their bed. Her eyes still filled with tears, she felt her way to the kitchen and found the telephone. Her fingers flew across the keypad as she dialed a number she had dialed countless times before.

Trinity picked up the phone on the first ring. "Hi, Dana! How are you?" she said, managing at once to be both friend and medical professional.

"Trin?" Nightcat stifled a sob. "It's David. He's ..."

"Oh, no, Dana. I'm so sorry. What happened?"

"I don't know. He just ... died. In bed. In his sleep, while I was out on my morning run."

"You stay where you are. I'll make all the phone calls, and we'll be there as soon as we can."

"Thanks, Trin," Nightcat said absently, and hung up the phone.

She wandered through the house, moving aimlessly from room to room and back again, everywhere except their bedroom. Finally, she could avoid it no longer. She walked slowly down the hall and into the bedroom, closing the door behind her. Sitting in the chair where David liked to sit and read before he went to bed, she rocked back and forth, sobbing uncontrollably.

Some time later she dried her eyes and looked toward the bed where David lay, his face towards her. She tried to tell herself he was just sleeping, that any minute he would get out of bed and stretch, and shave, and wash his face, and go to the kitchen to cook their breakfast. But she couldn't make herself believe it, not when all of her powerful senses told her David would never get up again, never smile at her again, never hold her in his arms again.

It had started as soreness in her chest which she thought was because of her crying, but it had grown, and now she recognized it for what it was. An icy calm asserted itself, as it had always done whenever Nightcat had found herself in a life and death situation. Swiftly she decided what she had to do.

She got up from the chair and went to her bedside table. From the drawer she took out a pen and a thin pad of note paper and scribbled a few lines. Crossing the room to the dresser, she retrieved a pair of pajama bottoms and a t-shirt from the bottom drawer and put them on the bed. Reaching into the back corner of the drawer, she fished out a small box and put it on the bed as well. Then she closed the drawer, sat down on the edge of the bed and composed herself in preparation for her most important task.

She had expected a struggle, a fight to impose her will on the nanites, but she reverted to her human form as easily as she had ever done. Her costume disappeared, replaced by the clothes she had been wearing when she had become Nightcat so many years before. She took these off, and slipped into the pajama bottoms and t-shirt, her favorite sleeping attire. She tossed her clothes into the laundry hamper; David didn't like it when she left them draped over a chair or, worse, lying on the floor.

Calmly she opened the box and took out a large studded collar. Part of her Nightcat costume, David had given it to her to replace the original, which she had lost during an epic battle early in her career. The collar was David's first gift to her, and in her mind the occasion had marked the official beginning of their relationship. She had not worn it since she and David had retired from crime-fighting. She set the note she had written on the bedside table and placed the collar on top of it.

With the last of her tasks completed, she pulled back the covers and crawled into the bed beside David. She tried to avoid contact with him for fear it would ruin the illusion that he was only asleep, but their bodies touched.

"You're so cold," she said, instinctively snuggling close and putting her arms around him to warm him with her body. She welcomed the darkness that pushed back the bright sunlight and spread slowly over the bedroom as she held him tightly, crying from the pain of her broken heart.

* * *

They were still there, together in their bed, two hours later when we arrived. After the police and the medical examiner had come and gone, and the paramedics had finally loaded my mother and father into an ambulance and driven away, my brother and I walked up the path to the woods. As soon as we were out of sight of the house, I changed to my cat form. He surprised me by changing forms as well; he rarely did so, never really having come to terms with this other side of his existence. Together we tracked my mother's last morning run, our enhanced senses making this task as easy as if she'd left us a map to follow. We remained in the forest for a time, taking turns stalking a very surprised wolf, until Trinity called us back to the house. Once there, it was not hard to piece together the remaining events of my parents' last few hours.

I have come back here often since that day. Initially, I came to hone my skills, to become more proficient in my cat form, but lately I have come back to experience the pure joy my second existence has to offer.

For my mother, who had it imposed upon her, it took many years before she began to accept her other self, and only near the end did she come close to being comfortable with it. But I was born so and have embraced it from the first day I discovered it within me. Apart from her love, it is the most cherished gift my mother gave me. I can think of only one way to repay her for this gift, and that is to be worthy of it. My mother was a reluctant, at times even unwilling superhero, but I gladly take up the task. I shall be her legacy.

In her note, my mother left to me the studded collar my father had given her as part of her costume. Since then it has been part of my costume, for now I am Nightcat.

Author Bios

J.L. MacDonald with her chorkie, Riley.
Photographer: Jode Kivol

J.L. MacDonald works as a full-time computer geek living in Saskatchewan, Canada with her personal zoo consisting of dogs, cats, rats, spiders and snakes. Highly influenced by superhero comics and cartoons in her youth, the idea of *Nightcat* first came to her when she was in her mid-teens. Some time later, Nightcat found her way onto virtual paper, appearing in several short stories and starring in a series of novels.

To learn more about Nightcat, visit http://nightcat.ca

Jim Robb is the controller of a multinational jewellery company. His stories have appeared in such diverse publications as AE, Sherlock Holmes Mystery Magazine, the children's anthology, "C is for Cabbage", and the Metahumans anthologies, two of which he co-edited with Jennifer MacDonald. He and his wife Donna live in southern Saskatchewan with their canine and feline associates.